About the Author

Lexie Winston has been an astronaut, rock star, princess and time traveller. In her dreams. But none of the dreams have lived up to what becoming an author has been like. She gets to live in a world of pure imagination, and her heroines get to do the things she's always wished she could.

When not writing books, Lexie is a mother of two gorgeous teenagers and the wife to a patient and understanding man. They live in Western Australia and are lorded over by a black toy poodle. She loves camping, reading and if her iPad was stolen, her world would explode. (It has the kindle app on it.) And you can find all links at

www.lexiewinston.com

Also by Lexie Winston

The Collectors Division

(Paranormal Reverse Harem Series)

Guardian

Guardian's Blood

Guardian Ascending

Collector's Division Omnibus

Neighpalm Industries Collective

(Enemies to Lovers Reverse Harem)

Abandoned Girl

Broken Girl

Tormented Girl

Wanted Girl

Cherished Girl

Loved Girl

Superficial Girl - Jacinta's Story Part 1

Superficial Girl - Jacinta's Story Part 2

Neighpalm Industries Collective 1-3

Neighpalm Industries Collective 4-6

Seductive Sins Collection

(Reverse Harem Series)

Glorious Gluttony

Gangs, Guns, and Glory

Glory Glory Hellelujah

Galaxy Circus

(Sci-Fi Reverse Harem Series)

Apprentice

Stagehand

Whisperer

Mama - Galaxy Circus Novella

Performer

Ringmaster

Interlude

A Night Most Wicked - Galaxy Circus Novella

Broken Promises

(Dark Poly Romance Series)

Secrets Kept

Lies Untold

Trust Broken

M.I.T.H.O.S

(Contemporary RH)

Spies Like Me

Storm View Stories

(Contemporary Standalone RH)

Ice Me Out

GLORY GLORY HELLELUJAH

Seductive Sins Series
Book 3

LEXIE WINSTON

NEIGHPALM
PUBLISHING

First published by Neighpalm Publishing in 2023

Glory Glory Hellelujah: Seductive Sins Series 3

Mobi format: 978-0-6453753-2-9
Print: 978-0-6453753-5-0
Cover design by Dazed Designs
Editing by Elemental Editing

Chapter One

"Are things always so crazy in your life?" Ben's tone holds a hint of accusation, and I guess with everything that's happened during our two interactions, I kind of can't blame him.

I push at his body, certain the danger has passed, and although I'm not too sad about feeling him pressed up against me, I'd like to get us away from the front yard. It certainly enforces the need for us to find somewhere else to be. I'm not entirely sure this problem won't follow us to Hell however. Despite being human, Bridgette seems to have a dozen resources at her disposal. It wouldn't surprise me one bit to find out she has some demon connection. I wonder if she knows Nolan and the girls are demons, and if this is something she knew previously or found out recently. There are so many things to unpack, but first, I want to get inside where it's a little safer.

Ben and I struggle to untangle ourselves, and Temple politely holds out the hand not holding the machine gun. When their hands meet, they both gasp, and I look down at their mate marks, each other's colors now wrapped around their own. Fuck my life, this is getting ridiculous. How many more men are going to end up in my mating circle? Why is this happening?

"Huh?" Ben looks perplexed, and Temple's mouth is wide with shock. "If I'm your mate, then how am I his mate as well?" Ben looks at me, and I huff out an exasperated sigh.

I shove at him, and he and Temple go back into action, dragging the man off me. Temple is still looking down at his hand when I clear my throat. He startles and looks down at me, his eyes wide and completely adorable. Ugh, seriously, all these men are going to ruin my vagina. What was fate thinking? Still, I hold my hand out, and when he takes it, it's as I expected. My palm stings with pain before my mark gathers another ring. It's starting to look a little like a rainbow now. That's six rings, six mates, and every single one of them is a different sin. The only one missing now is sloth, and why do I have the feeling that will eventually change?

Temple hauls me to my feet and reluctantly releases my hand. He's kind of gaping in shock, and I don't have the energy to deal with either of them and their conflicting emotions right this very second. I whirl around and almost burst into tears at the sight of our beautiful house. The front of it is riddled with bullet holes, windows are shattered, and there is glass lying all over the place. It's going to take forever to clean all this up, not to mention board up the windows and doors, so nothing and no one can enter uninvited.

A heavy hand lands on my shoulder, giving me a squeeze. "It looks bad, but it's nothing we can't fix." Temple's voice is a low rumble that's strangely comforting. "Why don't we go inside, so you can see that the girls and Louis are okay, and call your other mates before we get started?" he suggests, and I'm grateful as fuck, because Ben is less than useless. He's just muttering incoherently and staring at the mate mark, which is now as much of a rainbow as mine. How have we all ended up mated to each other? I could understand my first three mates, but the three new ones are also all mated to one another. I have never heard of such a thing outside of a lust demon's mating circle, and this is even more than most. My mother only has three, for fuck's sake.

"Yeah, okay." I nod gratefully. Toeing some of the glass out of the way of the front door, I carefully make my way inside. I want to sob when I take in the front living room. It's a mess of epic proportions too. I'm not sure what kind of gun it was, but it seems to have been high powered and had plenty of ammunition if the destruction is anything to go by. Thankfully Louis and the girls were still in the kitchen, and my mother had already left, otherwise, someone could have been easily killed. The furniture is also riddled with bullets, vases are smashed, the TV is destroyed, and the walls are filled with holes. I feel a tear trickle down my face, but sounds in the kitchen drag me away and straight toward my loved ones.

I find Louis with both girls in his arms, huddled down behind the kitchen island, protecting them both. The girls are crying hysterically, and he's trying to calm them with soothing words, but once they see me, they pull free of his hold and run for me.

"You're alive," Aria sobs as she throws herself at me, Zoe following quickly behind.

I sink to my knees and don't fight my tears any longer. I hug my girls and press kisses to their heads, so fucking grateful they are alive. I watch through teary eyes as Louis pulls his phone out of his pocket to call the other guys. The sounds of sirens reach my ears, and off to the side I see Temple and Ben joining us just as Mason hurries inside. He's breathing heavily, and he puts his hands on his knees, sucking in breaths.

"The cops are on their way. I tried to see who it was, but I wasn't fast enough," he says between harsh inhales.

"Did you chase them?" Temple asks, voicing what I was wondering.

"Yeah, as soon as the shooting started, I ran out the back door and around the house to see if I could catch the person, but as soon as you started returning fire, I had to duck so I wasn't hit. By the time I started moving again, they were gone." He sounds disappointed with himself, but I just stare at the man with amazement, unable to believe he chased a gunman for us.

"Thank you for trying," I tell him gratefully, and he nods, somber for a change.

"I'm just sorry I wasn't fast enough. If you don't mind, I'm going to stay out of the way when the cops are here. You don't need my presence confusing things." Of course, he's a wanted fugitive.

"That's fine. Head upstairs and find an empty bedroom," Louis tells him, clapping him on the shoulder. "Thank you for trying."

"Hey, I know this is new and all a bit up in the air, but I'm all in and take looking after our mate and children very seriously." There is no sign of the previously cheeky man. "I'm thrilled to be mated to Glory, and even more thrilled now that I know Temple is too." He must have felt and seen the new mate mark develop around his hand. When I look at it, I see he has all the rings now too.

Louis's eyes swing to Temple, and he nods his thanks. "Thank you as well."

Temple just grunts, but his frown softens.

Finally, Louis turns his attention to Ben. "I take it this is the other mate?"

I sigh, and Ben looks wide-eyed and shocked,

still staring down at all the colored rings around his demon mark. "Yes, this is Ben, but I'm not entirely sure he wants to be here." I hear the crackling of tires on the gravel driveway and know we are about to be surrounded by cops. Ben also doesn't dispute my comment, and I feel my stomach roll with nerves.

"Let's table this until after, okay? Head upstairs," I tell Mason. "Are you going to join him?" I ask Temple, not sure where he stands as far as the law goes. He is a known MC president.

"No, I'll stay. Someone will have to explain how we chased off the shooter," he replies, and I can't help but feel grateful.

"Hey, girls, why don't you help me find a bedroom?" Mason says to the two little girls who are still hiccupping in my arms. "I like to test a bed by jumping up and down on them to see if they are bouncy enough." This little bit of information quickly dries up the girls' tears as their interest piques.

Fuck, I seriously lucked out with five out of six of my mates. Mason is so sweet, trying to make the girls feel better. It does the trick, and both Aria and Zoe go with him after an encouraging nod from Louis and myself. By the time they get halfway up the spiral stairs, he has them giggling again. Ben trails absently after them. He's going to be a problem, but I don't have the energy to worry about that at the moment.

"Hello?" a voice calls from the front. "It's the police responding to a report of gunfire. Is everybody okay? Is anyone armed?" The voice is somewhat familiar, and I have a feeling it's one of the officers who attended the scene out at the cabin.

"We're in the kitchen and are unarmed," Louis calls back. Temple's gun has disappeared, so I'm assuming he returned it to wherever he retrieved it from previously.

We hear the crunching of glass as the officers make their way toward the kitchen. I hear one of them whistle. "Holy shit, it's a miracle no one was hurt or killed," he mutters, but our demon hearing is better than a human's, and all of us hear it. "It looks like a fucking gang zone in here."

They appear in the kitchen doorway, and I was right, I recognize the one in front from my abduction. "Ms. Luxure, is everyone okay?" He looks around the kitchen, a hand hovering over his gun. His eyes widen when he catches sight of Temple, but he doesn't go for his weapon.

"Yes, yes, the shooter got away. This is Louis and Temple. They were here with me when whoever it was started shooting," I tell the officers, but I don't go into detail about who they are. All they know is that I am Nolan Stephens' fiancée, and it was his ex-wife who kidnapped me.

"Do you have any clue whom it might have been?" the other officer asks, pulling out a notepad.

"Well, I guess the fact that a hit has been put out on me on the open market means it could have been almost anyone," I reply, shrugging. The two officers' eyes widen at that piece of information.

"A hit, really?" The one with the notebook can't quite believe my words. "Why would someone put a hit on you?" He sounds suspicious now and looks around the room like he's trying to find drugs or illicit goods.

"I'm the key witness to a kidnapping and attempted murder case. Unfortunately, the accused made bail and has disappeared." I go over to the fridge and pull out a bottle of wine as more tires crunch across the gravel. These ones are traveling a lot faster, and they come to a sudden stop. I'm going to guess that Carter and Nolan have arrived.

Sure enough, they come running into the kitchen, breathless and panicked. They look around, and I see them settle slightly as they notice we are unharmed, but I know they won't relax until they know everyone is okay. "The girls are upstairs, and they are fine," I tell them before they can ask.

"Thank fuck." Nolan strides over to me and yanks me into his arms. His strong grip and familiar smell go a long way to settling me even further. I kind of burrow in and soak up all his comfort, letting them talk over my head for a moment. Louis and Temple tell the two policemen, Carter, and Nolan exactly what happened.

"Bridgette will pay for this," Nolan mutters, and when I pull away from the comfort of his chest, I see his eyes blazing with his wrath demon. Thankfully, humans can't see the glow, so I don't have to worry about the police officers.

"We will put an APB out on Bridgette Weston, but I suggest you stay alert. We can't stop the hit that's been put on you, nor can we protect you from it." The officer frowns, folding his notebook closed.

"That's fine. We won't be staying here tonight, obviously. We're going to go somewhere that will be safer for all of us," Carter tells the two cops, who exchange a confused glance. Yes, I get it's confusing, but we don't have to explain anything to them.

"Please advise us of where you will be staying in case we need to contact you," he says as he tucks his notebook away.

"You can reach us through our lawyer. I'll grab his card." Nolan presses a kiss to my head and pulls away, tugging out his wallet and handing one of The Brad's cards to the first officer. "I'm sure you will understand why we don't want our location to be public knowledge."

"Yes, of course. We will make some inquiries into her location in the hopes that we can find her." The first officer takes the card.

Carter snorts indelicately. "I'm sure you'll understand if we do our own investigation."

They nod, giving a warning to stay within the boundaries of the law and then give their farewells. There's nothing they can do anyway.

We're all silent until we hear their car pull away. "Okay, we need to get out of here. We will go to the apartment above the club for tonight. There's a private entrance we can use so the girls don't have to walk through the club. We'll make arrangements to go to Hell tomorrow," Nolan says the minute they are out of earshot. "I'll beg Lucifer if I need to."

"Well, considering that you're mated to his niece, I'm not sure begging is going to be necessary. I guess it all depends on whether he's forgiven his sister or is holding a grudge," Louis says dryly, nodding in my direction.

"Mom seemed determined to go by herself and beg for his forgiveness. Let's hope what they say about him isn't true." I grab the broom from the walk-in pantry and head toward the front of the house, wanting to clean up.

"You know he doesn't punish souls, right?" Temple asks as I brush past him, and I feel the rest of them follow behind me.

He takes the broom from my hand and begins sweeping up the broken glass on the porch. Louis holds a dustpan and brush, and he starts sweeping bits of porcelain and glass up off the carpet. Carter gathers some of the destroyed cushions before taking them outside to the trash, as Nolan pulls down ruined picture frames.

"He isn't anything more than a king and punishes his own citizens, but he has nothing to do with the human realm."

"To be honest, I wasn't really sure. Every time we asked about the demon realm, our fathers shut us down. I guess I now know why." I look around the room, and while what the guys are doing is helping, nothing short of getting rid of the furniture is going to make it better.

"Do you have anything to board up the windows with?" Temple asks once he's swept all the glass on the porch into a pile, which Louis gathers to put in the trash.

"Yeah, in the shed out back. They are left over from when we built this place." Louis gestures in the direction of the backyard.

"Come on, I'll show you," I tell him, feeling kind of useless.

"Mason!" he calls out, and within moments, the man in question runs down the stairs. I look in the direction he came from, but before I can ask where the girls are, he holds up his hands.

"They are okay. Ben is teaching them some dance moves from part of his show."

"Ben?" Nolan and Carter have joined us, and they look confused.

"Poppy Cox arrived just before the shooting started," I explain, and their confusion clears.

"Come on, let's grab those boards. I don't think it would be a good idea to hang around much longer." Temple walks down the steps, and Mason and I follow him.

"Why don't you go pack some bags for us?" I suggest to my other guys.

"Good thinking. None of us keep a house in Hell anymore, so we need to take everything with us." Louis blows me a kiss and heads back into the house.

"What about you guys?" Nolan asks Temple and Mason. "I'm sure between Carter and me, we can find you something to wear."

Mason smiles. "Thanks, but I keep a house in Hell, and we both have things there. Unfortunately, though, it's not big enough for all of us to stay there." He blushes slightly, which is a weird look on the previously confident man.

"Don't sweat it. There are hotels. I'll book us something. That's what we did in the past when we went home to visit family," Carter reassures him. Visit family? Does this mean I'm going to find out about the guys' families? It's been such a whirlwind that we haven't really had a chance to talk about theirs, except for Bella.

"Let's get this taken care of then, shall we? Standing here, so exposed, is making me nervous." My eyes dart around the rapidly darkening front yard. There are so many trees, anyone could be hiding amongst them, not to mention someone sitting on the wall surrounding the place like the last person.

Chapter Two

"So you want to tell us what this is all about?" Mason jogs after me as I head toward the shed out back with Temple. We could have tried to conjure everything, but with our mating circle all over the place, and three out of the six bonds unsealed, I don't think any of us wanted to risk something going wrong.

I still don't understand how I went from three mates less than twelve hours ago to double that now, and they are all mated to each other. I don't know of any other mating circle that's like that. My dads are all just mated to my mom, or I'm almost certain they are. I haven't ever seen them show romantic affection toward each other, just brotherly regard.

"Long story short, the girls' mother is a money hungry bitch, and when her attempt to manipulate Nolan failed, she resorted to kidnapping. She quickly learned not to mess with a demon trying to protect her kids, but she's out on bail, and I guess she wants to get rid of the only witness to her crimes. Unlike the two idiots we caught at the drag show, I can put a face and voice to a name. They never met her face-to-face."

"And she doesn't care if her daughters get caught in the cross fire? That's one cold bitch," Mason sounds as disgusted as I felt when Temple told us that. I wouldn't be sad if it was her who was shooting at us and she got hit by one of Temple's bullets. I'm certain it wasn't, though, because she wouldn't risk being caught, and whoever it was drove away after, so I'm guessing they survived.

I feel exhausted as I push open the door to the shed and flick on the light, looking around. I bet all that gunfire scared off the delivery dude, and I'm going to have to wait even longer for food. Now that's just the icing on top of a shit cake. It's been such a long freaking day, and every new mate has sapped a little bit more energy. I'm surprised I haven't burst into flames, or maybe I am so low on energy I can't even do that.

I wobble slightly, but a hand at the base of my spine steadies me. "Hey, why don't you go back to the house? Mason and I have this. It won't take us long. If you're all packed and ready, we can leave as soon as you're done." Temple's large hand is solid and reassuring against my back, and he's saying all the right words. I'm done with today. I need a good meal and my bed for a solid ten hours before I can even think about everything that today has brought me, so I'm not going to argue.

"Thanks, you have no idea how much I appreciate it," I tell him, and Mason's face brightens with a smirk.

"I'm sure you can show us both how much once things have settled a little." He winks, and I can't help but smile at his ridiculous behavior. I appreciate him trying to distract me.

"I'll see you both back at the house," I tell them without engaging Mason and make my way back to the house, my brain swirling with all of today's events—my mother's information about her brother, Lucifer, and their falling out, my three new mates, and the hit taken out on me. I have no idea how we're going to deal with all of this. I almost wish I hadn't ever said anything about my life being boring. The universe obviously took it to heart and threw everything it could at me.

My cell starts to ring just as I approach the back door to the house. I can hear Louis and Carter talking in the kitchen, so I stop and fish it out of my cargo pants. It's my dad, and I want to check if Mom made it home okay, so I don't send it to voicemail.

"Hey, Dad," I greet as I accept the call. "Did Mom make it home okay?" I make my voice a little brighter in the hopes he doesn't ask what's wrong, but his deep sigh instantly has me on alert.

"She's here, but she's talking about going to Hell to see her brother and making things right.

Something about needing to help you. None of us can get her to stop for a moment and take a breath."

"Ah, yeah, she said she was going to smooth things over with him so he can help us with a little problem we're having," I tell him, not sure if I should go into too many details. I don't need my dads worrying, and I'm sure Mom will tell them anyway when she calms down.

"She did tell you why you didn't know that Luc was her brother and why we haven't been to Hell since we've been mated, right?"

"She said something about being tricked by an old boyfriend and being ashamed about her reaction." I frown, taking a seat on the porch step, unsure where my dad is going with this.

He sighs again, but this time it's even heavier. "Luc has no children, and because of this, he named your mother as his heir. Demons are long-lived, and Luc has been ruler for a long time, so he is ready to hand the mantle over. The reason we haven't returned is because if we do, she will have to take over the leadership role from her brother, and we will be confined to Hell. I love your mother, but she isn't suited for being in charge of a household, let alone a whole country."

He's not wrong. My mom is loving and kind, but she's also flighty, forgetful, and indecisive. She uses a magic eight ball for all her important decisions.

"If that's the case, then why hasn't he sent his own bounty hunters after her?" I know Kerry's dad works for Lucifer in this capacity.

"Because despite their falling out, he loves his little sister, and he wants her to come of her own volition. Now that you, Serena, and the boys are more settled, she is happy to sacrifice herself, but we really can't let her." My heart sinks, and I know our plan is going to have to change.

"Fuck, Dad!" I exclaim and rub my face with my spare hand. "I'm stuck between a rock and a hard place. I guess we can go hide out in Hell somewhere else. One of my new mates has a place there, and Carter said they usually stay in hotels. We can keep a low profile and hope that Lucifer doesn't find out we're there. I was hoping to ask him for his help in locating the girls' mother, who seems to have disappeared, but I'm sure we can figure out something else."

He simultaneously thanks me and apologizes before we hang up, and I hang my head. I have no clue what we're going to do now. Padding footsteps and a wet tongue across my cheek have me reaching out and burying my face in Max's fur as a few unstoppable tears trickle down my face. He sits on his haunches as he patiently waits for me to have my silent breakdown.

I can't wallow for too long, though, because Mason and Temple will be returning shortly, and I still need to pack a bag and make sure everyone else is ready to go. Wiping my eyes on his shaggy fur, I pull away, giving him a scratch on his scruff. "Thanks for not judging, buddy," I tell him, and he just smiles his doggy grin at me, his tongue hanging out and tail wagging. I wonder if we can take him to Hell with us or if I should arrange for my brothers to look after him for a few days. I'm not sure how long we'll be gone, so it might be better that he stays here so we don't have to worry about him on the other plane.

I stand up and stretch, shoving my phone back into the pocket on my cargos. I actually know nothing about Hell except it's a different plane where demons originate from. There's Heaven too, and angels who are just like demons but have wings, and their personalities are based on the seven heavenly virtues. They have the same kind of powers, but from what I understand, that plane has been inaccessible for a long time.

Demons like to come to Earth to feed off humans' sins while unmated, but they return to Hell once mated, or most of them do anyway. Angels have no need for that. Apparently, they believe they are superior to both demons and humans and won't demean themselves by associating with either race.

That's fine with me, I don't think we need any more self-righteous assholes in our world. Earth has enough of them.

I can't avoid my problems any longer. I hear Aria and Zoe inside, asking where I am, so I make the decision to tackle one issue at a time, and right now, getting us to a safer location is the most pressing problem. I open the door and step into the kitchen. My three bonded mates are there as well as the two girls. They all stop talking when they see me. There are four large duffle bags on the island bench, and there's one empty one sitting on the floor.

Nolan smiles at me as I enter, but I can see the clouds of worry in his eyes. "There you are. This is for you." He hands me the empty bag. "We weren't sure what you wanted to take, so we left it for you. Why don't you run upstairs and pack a few things while we load the car?"

I notice someone is missing. "Where's Ben?" I ask, and Louis winces.

"He left. His car was undamaged in the cross fire, and he muttered something about needing to think."

"Oh." I can't help but sound disappointed. I mean, I was surprised to discover I had more mates, but he genuinely seemed disappointed, and I'm woman enough to admit that hurts.

"Go easy on him, Glory. I think he's a little younger than us. I guess this is all a bit of a shock to him." Carter gets off his stool and pulls me in for a hug. I take a moment to breathe him in and accept the offered comfort.

"I liked him. He promised to show me how to paint pretty things on my nails," Zoe declares from where she's sitting at the island bench. When I pull away from Carter to smile at the two girls, I notice their hair has been styled into elaborate braids that I couldn't manage without many tears and YouTube videos.

"Did he do your hair?" I ask the girls, and Aria nods.

"Yes, he said he loved playing with hair when he was younger, and he learned it when doing his girlfriend's hair." She frowns. "If he has a girlfriend, then why was he here to see you?" she asks, and I'm kind of stumped for words. I look to their father for help, and he doesn't let me down.

"Well, you know how we explained that Glory has three boyfriends?"

"Yes, you three," Zoe shouts, pointing to three men before clapping.

"Well, it turns out she has three more as well, and Ben is one of those."

"Why was he talking about girlfriends then?" Aria bites her lip with worry.

"I think he meant girlfriends from when he was still in school," Louis assures her.

"And why did he leave then, and who are the other two boyfriends?" She's certainly full of questions tonight, but I know it's because she doesn't like to be surprised. So much of her early childhood was spent dodging Bridgette's mood swings and whims, so she likes to have her ducks all in a row now.

I head over to her and wrap my arms around her, giving her the comfort I know she needs. "I'm not sure why he left, but I'm sure he had good reasons. This has been a bit of a shock to all of us, and we all deal with surprises in different ways," I tell her gently as she leans her head against me.

"As for the other two boyfriends, that would be me and him." A voice at the door leading to the living room has us all turning to look. Mason and Temple are both standing there.

"Yay!" Zoe cheers and bounces up and down on her chair, and even Aria smiles a little brighter.

"Well, I guess that's out there now," I mutter, pulling away from Aria. "Did you get the windows boarded up?" I look at Temple because he seems to be the more responsible one despite whatever their bedroom dynamics may be.

"Yes, everything is secure. Oh, and the food was delivered while we were out there. I tipped the driver extra because he looked kind of terrified when he saw all the bullet holes in the side of the house. I'm hoping that may help him come back in the future." He holds up two huge plastic bags full of takeaway containers, and my stomach rumbles loud enough for everyone to hear it.

There's a pause of silence before everyone laughs loudly, the tension broken by my starving body.

"Thank you." Louis walks over and takes the bags from him. "Come on, let's eat and then we can get out of here. The apartment above the club has three bedrooms, and it's secure enough for us to stay overnight. We will take a portal to Hell tomorrow. After a good night's sleep, things won't look so bad in the morning."

"And we have our most experienced team looking for Bridgette. We might wake up tomorrow, and she'll be found, and then we can just come home." Nolan gets some plates out as Louis starts pulling the containers out of the bags. I gesture for Mason and Temple to join us at the island. We have a big table in the dining room, but that just means extra time before I can eat. I'm happy standing and leaning against a wall with a bowl of food in my hand.

Carter opens the fridge and pulls out a few beers, passing them around. I shake my head when he offers me one, but the guys all accept. He pours the girls small glasses of juice as well. "I've organized for your brothers to meet us at the club. They are going to take Max home when they finish their shifts tonight," Carter tells me, and I remember something.

"We never did discuss why they were there," I point out as Louis fills a plate of food before passing it to me. Nolan does the same for both girls before all five men prepare their own.

Carter shrugs. "They needed jobs, and we had places for them. Callen and Kade will take the next course, and if they are good, which I'm sure they will be, then they will join Wrathful Bail Bonds, and Silas and Seth will take over the majority of club management for the time being, freeing us both up to spend more time with you. Tasty Treats will be the only business we have to concentrate on for now."

"And I have new managers in place whom I am super happy with," Louis says before taking a swig of his beer. "Getting rid of Nicole and Jenny was the best thing for our business. I didn't realize how terrible they were at their jobs. An older German couple, retired bakers, applied, and they are perfect."

It couldn't be the two who helped me out on that first day at Tasty Treats, could it? Shaking my head, I concentrate on the food in front of me. The guys have all made arrangements to free themselves up, which is amazing, and I know that financially we can afford it, but when everything dies down, I'm not certain we won't all drive each other mad if we are constantly in one another's pockets. That's a future Glory problem, though, I'll worry about that once we have sorted out our current issues. For now, food is my biggest focus.

Chapter Three

Dinner is a fairly subdued affair. I desperately want to question Mason and Temple and get to know them, but now really isn't the time, and with little ears around, I can't really ask them about their former lives as a thief and MC president. I'm also not sure what they are going to do now that those options are closed for them.

"You know we could add a security consultant offshoot to Wrathful Bail Bonds," I muse out loud once we've all finished eating and are cleaning up.

The girls ran upstairs to make sure they have everything they want, but the five guys stop and stare at me like I lost my mind.

I wave my hand at them, encouraging them to keep going. "I was just thinking about what Mason and Temple are going to do now that their former professions are kind of off the table, and a former thief would be good at assessing if someone's security system is up to scratch."

"And Temple happens to be quite the computer whiz." Mason nods, pointing at his partner, jumping on my idea without hesitation.

"I think the term you're looking for is hacker," Temple scoffs as he bends over and places his plate in the dishwasher.

"Really?" I can't help but sound skeptical as the big man stands up to his full height. There is nothing about him that says computer nerd.

He blushes a little and shrugs. "I was a late bloomer. I was super skinny and smart as a teenager, and I was picked on by the bigger kids. To make myself less of a target, I learned how to hack into the school system and change grades for a fee. It kept me safe, and I discovered I had a knack for it. My stepfather discovered my skills and wanted to make use of them, so he found me a mentor. The man who taught me was the biggest cyber thief the world had ever seen, and he still hasn't been caught, so I became proficient in cybercrime."

"Such a lackluster word for your skills." Mason winks at him before turning back to me. "But it's exactly the type of thing needed for a security consultant business."

"Is that how you found out who put the hit on Glory?" Nolan asks. "Because those dark web notice boards are typically anonymous."

Temple nods. "Yeah, it really wasn't that difficult."

"I like that idea. Those skills will also come in handy with Wrathful Bail Bonds as well." Carter claps Temple on the back.

Thankfully, my three bonded mates have been super accepting of the new ones. It could have been a disaster if jealous Carter had shown up again. I guess he is secure in his place now so there's no need for him to be an asshole.

"Okay, let's get this show on the road." Louis dries his hands on a dishtowel after he turns the dishwasher on.

Crap, I still haven't packed. I run upstairs as Nolan calls to the girls who come down. I pass them on the steps. They are carrying backpacks and their teddies from Build-A-Bear. "Let the guys put you into the car, I won't be long," I assure them. It's almost their bedtime, and I can see their eyes starting to droop. They'll probably fall asleep in the car on the way.

It doesn't take me long to throw some clothes into the empty duffle bag—mostly jeans and shirts, but I also include a nicer dress or two just in case. The guys assure me Hell has shops if we leave anything behind. When I asked about money, they explained that Hell has its own currency, but we can exchange American dollars for it when we get there. Lastly, I add my toiletries, and I'm good to go.

I hurry out into the garage. We're taking two vehicles—the Wrathful Bail Bonds truck and Nolan's SUV with the girls' car seats in it. I pass Carter my duffle bag, which he packs into the back of the SUV, and climb into the passenger seat.

Louis is driving this one with me, the girls, and Max, who is securely strapped in between them, and the other four are riding in the truck. Nolan starts it as Carter sets the house alarm. I'm not sure it's worth it with the board-covered windows, but I guess it doesn't hurt.

We are finally on our way, and I can't stop the sigh of relief that slips from my mouth. "Seriously, the sooner we can get to Hell, the safer I'll feel about all of this," I quietly tell Louis.

"What about Ben?" It's Aria who asks this quiet question as we pull down the driveway and out onto the street, our house fading into the distance behind us.

Louis and I exchange a glance, but neither of us have an answer for her. "He has Daddy's number, so if he wants to reach out and find where we are, he can." I turn around to look at her in the passing streetlights. Zoe's eyes are already closed, and I can tell by her quiet snuffling that she's fast asleep. "We can't force someone to be a part of our family, they have to want to be here," I say gently, and a little frown forms between her eyes.

"Is it because of me? Does he not want kids?" My heart breaks for the poor girl. Traumatized by her mother, this is her default reaction.

"Oh, honey, no. This all happened so quickly. I'm sure Ben has a lot of things to think about. It has nothing to do with you at all. Remember, he was happy to hang out with you earlier," I remind her, and her frown clears.

"Okay. I hope he decides he wants to be a part of our family. I think he needs us. He seemed kind of sad too."

"He did, didn't he?" I can't help but agree with Aria. Below the glitz and glamor, there seemed to be a lost little boy. I can only hope that we are exactly what he needs, but like I said to Aria, he needs to make that decision himself.

The drive to the club takes about half an hour. Nolan and the other guys are somewhere behind us as Louis pulls into a private, underground parking lot. He pulls into a parking space not far from an elevator.

"That's our private entrance. Come on, you get Zoe, and I'll grab Aria. Max will follow, and the other guys will bring up everything else." He turns the car off, and we get out, carefully unstrapping the girls without waking them and lifting them into our arms for the trip up to the apartment.

Louis juggles Aria in his arms and swipes a key card across the inside of the elevator, activating it. There are three buttons as well as one labeled as parking. He presses the top one.

"The top is the apartment, the middle is the dance club, and the bottom button is the sex club," he explains as the elevator starts to move upward.

"Do we have to worry about the girls getting

down there in the morning?" I ask him quietly, and he shakes his head.

"No, they need to swipe that card before it will go anywhere. The dance club closes during the day, but the sex club is twenty-four seven, and we don't want anyone to be able to use this elevator without permission."

We stop moving, and the doors open. I was worried we would hear the thumping bass from the dance club up here, but there isn't a sound except for my and Louis's shoes on the hardwood floors and the hum of a refrigerator.

Lights activate as we walk farther into the apartment, so they must be motion activated. Louis leads the way past an open kitchen, dining, and living room and then down a small hallway.

"Each bedroom has an attached bathroom, and there's a hot tub on the balcony," he tells me quietly as he pushes a door open. "Mostly the three of us share the main bedroom, but like the house, we have our own rooms. This is mine." He steps farther into the dark room, and I see him bend over and place Aria onto the bed. He presses the button on a small bedside lamp, and a shadowy illumination brightens the room slightly.

His room is very basic, with the walls and furnishing in neutral shades. I go around to the other side and place Zoe on the bed before taking her shoes and socks off and putting them next to the bed. Both of them changed into pj's before we left, so all that's left to do is maneuver them so we can cover them with the blankets. Once they are covered, I press a kiss to Zoe's forehead, whispering for her to sleep well, before going around and doing the same for Aria. Max, who has obediently trailed behind us, makes himself comfortable at the foot of their bed, letting out a doggy huff of air as he gets comfortable.

Louis leaves the lamp on, and we exit the room, leaving the door open in case either girl wakes in the night and needs us.

"That's Carter's." He points to the door directly across the hall. "Mason and Temple can have that, and we'll share the master." He waves his hand at the door at the very end of the corridor. "But let's go wait for the others. Are you still hungry? You're looking a little pale. Is everything okay?"

We make it back to the living room, and I throw myself onto one of the large sofas. I have to say one thing for my mates, they have fantastic taste in furniture. Everything is big and soft and comfy. "I don't know, I feel off balance, like at any moment, someone is going to start shooting at us. I'm also a little lightheaded and unfocused. I don't like it."

He sits down next to me, his large hand coming up to cup my face. "Oh, my little dumpling, a lot has occurred in the last twenty-four hours. It's no wonder you are feeling off balance." He picks up my hand and turns it over so we can both look at all the colored rings around my own demon designation. "Six mates are a lot to adjust to. I'm sure once you seal the bond with the other three, everything will stabilize. Now, how about I get you a glass of wine, and we'll see what we can find for you to eat. You didn't really eat as much as you need at dinner." He raises a questioning eyebrow.

"No," I admit. "As hungry as I am, my stomach won't settle enough to enjoy it, and it's not doing a damn thing to make me feel any better. It's Bella's wedding all over again and an aching hunger that can't be fixed."

Before he can respond, the elevator opens and lets Nolan and Carter in, each carrying two duffle bags with two more at their feet. Nolan drops his two and goes back for the others before allowing the elevator to close. "Where are the other two?" I ask, unable to hide the disappointment in my tone, and I have no idea why I feel that way. How is it that I've grown attached to practical strangers so quickly?

"I suggested that they should have a drink at the bar and that I would send you down to join them," Carter tells me, coming over and pressing a kiss to my head before continuing down the hallway to the last door.

"Why?" I call after him before turning my confusion on Nolan. "Why would he do that?"

"Because, babe, three more mate bonds snapped into place today. That has to be riding you pretty hard." He leans against one of the kitchen counters and crosses his arms. "We all talked about it, and we think it would be smart for you to seal the bonds with those two immediately. Just like you did with us."

"But I barely know them," I argue, and Nolan shrugs unsympathetically as Carter returns to the living room, minus his bags.

"You barely knew us either. It's the way of the mate bond. It doesn't care, you know that. Until they are locked into place, you're going to be unstable, and that would be a bad thing while traveling to Hell." He sits down across from us and leans forward, propping his elbows on his knees.

"But I thought you said Hell was just a normal place like Earth," I argue, and Louis scoffs.

"Yes and no, but the population is made entirely of demons, and they've never been afraid to test someone, especially once the word gets out that you are Lucifer's niece. Matings can be challenged."

"I'm sorry, what did you say? I don't think I heard you right. Challenged?" I can't believe he's telling me this.

"Yes, until a mating circle is completely sealed, you can be challenged for your mates. You have to prove you're worthy, and if you lose, the winner can petition Lucifer to dissolve the mating, but usually the power of Hell takes over and does it anyway," Carter says, speaking like he's not imparting life-changing information.

"The power of Hell?" I sound like a parrot now, but I can't help it, all of this new information is blowing my mind.

"Yes, it's where all of our powers originate from. Think of Hell as a sentient being with whims and moods, and it respects and acknowledges strength and fighting for what you want." Nolan pushes off the counter and goes to the fridge, digging around inside it and pulling out three beers. He opens the three of them, twisting the tops violently before distributing them to the guys.

"I can't believe the three of you are being so casual about this!" I sound whiny and pathetic. Nolan takes a seat next to Carter and sighs like he's settled in for the night, but in my defense, I'm hungry and out of sorts.

"Glory, there's no point in fighting this. Go seal your bonds with two more of your mates." Louis is the one who finally responds after the three of them exchange loaded glances.

I stand up, throwing my hands into the air. "What's the point if I'm going to be challenged for them anyway when I get to hell?" I'm pissed now, and they can tell. "How many exes have you three left in your wake? Am I going to have problems?" The next shared glance is even heavier than the last. "Fuck my life."

"Well, Temple is probably in the clear. Like you, he's never been to Hell, but I'm afraid the rest of us have spent plenty of time there. I'm not sure about Ben, so we'll have to ask him if he ever reappears," Carter admits, sounding more than appropriately sheepish.

"Fucking fabulous. If it were up to me right this second, I'd be letting Hell take you all. What the fuck did I do to deserve ending up with man whores as mates?" I mutter as I turn my back on them and head to the elevator. I consider showering and putting on something a little sexier, but fuck it. If we're going to be together, then they are going to see me at my worst, so I may as well start with how I intend to go on.

I stab the button to call the elevator, but it must not have returned downstairs, because the doors open immediately. I step in and turn back around to face my mates.

"In our defense, all demons are man and lady whores," Carter calls, but I ignore him.

"Have fun, sweetie," Louis says, forever trying to keep the peace, but I just throw up my middle finger, and as the doors close, I hear them chuckle.

Assholes! Once the doors close completely, I feel a smile creep across my lips. Yes, it's a little fast, but I can't deny I'm excited to see Temple and Mason together, and hopefully, they will invite me to play too.

Chapter Four

W hen the doors open to the club, the music is loud, and the dance floor is crowded. I head straight to the bar and wave down Silas, my brother. He waves and finishes serving the person in front of him before walking in my direction with a worried frown on his face.

"Hi, Glory." He leans over the bar and gives me a kiss on the cheek. "Are you okay? Carter called me earlier and told me about what went down at your place. Are Zoe and Aria okay?"

My brothers are a huge pain in my ass, as brothers are, but they are good boys, and it's sweet that Silas is worried about the girls. They've wrapped all four of my brothers around their little fingers in a very short period of time.

"Yes. Thankfully they were both in the kitchen and the bullets didn't go farther than the living room," I reply as he grabs a bottle of gin and pours me a large gin and tonic before sliding it over to me. "Shit, I didn't bring my purse down," I tell him, and his worry clears, and he chuckles.

"Sis, you're mated to the owners. I'm pretty sure anything you want is on the house."

"Huh, I had forgotten about that." I feel a little silly now that he mentioned it and hide my embarrassment by looking around for Mason and Temple. They are both big guys, so they should be easy to spot, but I can't see them anywhere.

"Are you looking for someone?" my brother asks, and I look back at him and nod. He fishes around in his apron and pulls out a folded note before handing it to me.

"Met my new brothers-in-law earlier. They asked me to give you this." My annoying brother doesn't wait for a response before he leaves to serve another person farther down the bar.

The note he slid across the bar feels like a snapping turtle waiting to bite my fingers off, but despite my trepidation, there's a part of me that wants—no, needs to know what the note says. Taking a breath, I reach out and flip it open with one finger. Two words are written on it. Well, a word and a number. *Room 5.* I take a sip of my gin and tonic, wincing at the strength of the gin as I stare at the note, trying to decide if I'm going to be brave or hide my head in the sand and go back up to the apartment.

Pfft, who am I kidding? I've never shied away from a challenge. Yeah, I don't know either of these men, but fate has decided they are mine, or ours, I guess. I'm not sure what's going to happen with the other guys, and whether they will be happy to stay in their own throuple or invite Mason and Temple into their beds too, but that's up to them. Secretly, my vote is for one huge freaking orgy, but that's for another day. Today it's just the three of us.

I quickly drink the rest of my gin and tonic—a little liquid courage never hurt anyone—before placing the glass back on the bar. I wave to my brother who smirks and gives me a nod, not stopping what he's doing. It's weird seeing him without his twin, but then I realize I may very well see too much of his twin when I head downstairs. Fuck, that would suck. Sighing, I weave my way into the crowd. I catch sight of Kade standing on a box so he can see across the top of all the people on the dance floor. He gives me a nod and wink but doesn't turn his attention away from the crowd. It takes me a bit to get to the public elevator to get downstairs, due to the sheer number of people inside the club, but I eventually make it there and only get felt up twice by wandering hands. I'm calling that a win.

As I approach the elevator, a muscular bouncer steps between me and my destination. "I'm sorry, ma'am, this is a members only elevator. You need a membership card to access it."

Fuck, why didn't I think of that? Of course I

don't have a card. I should have grabbed one of the guys'.

"Would you mind swiping me down? I left mine upstairs in the apartment." I flutter my eyelashes at him, but he doesn't even crack a smile, just snorts in disbelief.

"You're expecting me to believe you came from the owners' apartment upstairs? I'm sorry, but the bosses never take their dates upstairs." He says "dates" like it's a dirty word, and I scowl at him.

"Well, I'm relieved to hear that, but considering I'm engaged to them, I would think I would be welcome." I lift my left hand and waggle my engagement ring at him, but he doesn't look impressed.

"Please, do you know how many times that's been tried with me?" He rolls his eyes and grabs my arm. "Please move away from the elevator, or I'm going to have to remove you from the club."

Right, that's fucking it. This dude just pushed my last fucking button, and I'm about to open a can of whoop ass on him. If only I had Sparky, but the guys make me leave it in the lockbox of their truck. I yank my arm out of his hold.

"Take your fucking hands off me. You have five seconds to use that radio in your ear and ask someone above you if Gloriana Luxure is engaged to the owner before I shove my fist down your throat and pull out your fucking heart." I can feel the wrath ring around my mate mark start to burn, and I'm shocked when I look at the mirrored surface of the elevator and see that my eyes are glowing red like Nolan's do. Whoa, that's new.

This guy has obviously been hit in the head one too many times, though, because he doesn't take my warning to heart. He uses the radio, but I hear him alert the staff that he has a hostile and is preparing for a takedown.

The dude better bring it, because he's going to be unemployed and not walking by the time I'm done with him.

"Hey, whoa, hang on," a voice calls out over the crowd, and I watch as Kade manhandles the crowd out of his way just as the beefy dude grabs for my arm again. It's like it happens in slow motion, but I shove his hand out of the way, making mine into a fist, and thrust it into his throat. The guy's eyes bug out, and he gasps for air and doubles over, my throat punch rendering him incapable of much of anything.

"Fuck, Glory." Kade reaches my side and looks at the asshole without sympathy. "I tried to tell him, but the fucker wouldn't listen."

"Well, he'll be sorry about that when he can finally breathe and discover that he's been fired. All he had to do was make some inquiries or even listen to you. Hopefully he will listen better on the next job."

"Fuck you, bitch," the guy in front of us gasps, and I haul back and kick him between the legs. Nobody speaks to me like that.

"Shit, Glory, stop." Kade pulls me away from the now fetal position bouncer as two more approach us from the dance floor. I whirl on my brother, stabbing a finger into his chest.

"You have no idea the kind of day I've had. I have been shot at twice, gained three more mates, and have a hit out on me that isn't concerned with the girls getting caught in the cross fire. I'm starving and unstable, and he was the straw that broke the camel's back."

Kade's eyes widen, and he grabs my face between his hands. "Whoa, Glory, your eyes are red. That's not normal," he tells me. "I think I should call Nolan down."

"Just swipe the elevator for me. I don't have a card, and I need to go downstairs, please." I'm desperate and not above begging my brother for help.

"Without your mates?" he frowns with disappointment, and I feel the urge to throat punch him, but it's kind of sweet that my brothers are already attached to my mates.

"I have two new ones who are waiting for me down there to seal the bond," I tell him, and he grimaces, looking slightly green.

"I didn't need to know that," he mutters before

pulling a card out of his pocket. "Go, I'll deal with this mess." The other two bouncers look like they don't know whether to grab me or wait. Kade waves them back. "I'll be up at the end of my shift to grab Max and take him home with us."

"The other guys are up there. I'm not sure if I'll be done by then," I tell him as the door opens and I step in.

He sighs and closes his eyes. "TMI," he mutters, and I just roll my eyes at him as the doors close.

Fuck, my brothers are prudes. Mom and Serena used to talk work all the time at the dinner table, and my brothers would always get up and leave. Pussies. How are they going to cope with working in a sex club? Maybe that's why Kade is upstairs.

The elevator is blessedly silent as it makes its way down to the next level. I'm not sure if I'm nervous or still agitated from that encounter, but I'm twitchy and restless. I think I'll have another quick drink to settle myself before heading to the room.

The doors open to a large, open space. Last time I was here, it was filled with half naked people, some of them fucking on the dance floor—or that's what I remember the most. I wasn't in my right mind due to the devil dust.

This time, though, there is a scene being played out in the middle of the open space, and people are standing around watching it. I look a little closer, and it's a woman tied to a St. Andrew's cross. At her feet is another woman with her head bowed, who's kneeling with her hands on her knees, perfectly submissive. Both are wearing scraps of lingerie and serene smiles on their faces. To one side is a mostly naked dude wearing a mask on his face, and he has a leather flogger in one hand, but it's the tattoo on the back of his thigh that has me wrinkling my nose and turning away from the action.

Fuck me, having my brother as the dungeon master is going to make this place off-limits. We're going to have to stick to the playroom at home. I need to show Temple and Mason where that is, because I don't need to see my brother getting his freak on. Yes, I know I just accused Kade of being a prude, but hearing about it is one thing, and seeing it is on a whole other level.

Thankfully the bar down here is hidden off to the side, so I won't have a view of the main floor. I wave down the bartender, and this time it's Callen.

"Hey, sis." He leans over and gives me a kiss.

"I thought you were bouncing down here," I say, taking a seat. Most of the stools are empty as everyone seems to be enjoying the show.

He fake gags and shakes his head. "Not when Seth is putting on a show. No thanks."

I chuckle. "Yeah, I was just thinking the same thing. Can I get the largest, strongest cocktail you have? But no devil dust. Mom's genes are too strong, and the dust wreaks havoc on my system. I need a clear head."

"Yeah, after your reaction last time, we all decided it would be best to avoid it. Unless we are here, having fun." He winks, and it's my turn to fake gag.

"I'm surprised there is anyone left for you to have sex with," I comment. My brothers are notorious man-whores. Huh, maybe there is some stock to the comment Carter made earlier.

"Ah, but now we have a whole new selection. Demons are more fun, and they don't expect commitment like all the human girls from school, not to mention the humans they allow down here are interested in having a very good time—no prudish sensibilities to be seen. It's freaking awesome."

"Well, you make sure it's all safe and consensual. We don't need any rape accusations or claims of you being a baby daddy just yet. Not to mention you have a mate out there somewhere. I'm sure they will be thrilled to find out their mate was a man whore before they met them," I say, not hiding my sarcasm. I'm intimately familiar with how it feels, so I believe I am looking out for their future mates by pointing it out.

He blanches slightly. "Yeah, okay, you make a fair point, but hopefully that's still years away. Look at you, you're old and only now finding your mates.

I'd say I have a good ten years at least." He grins as he mixes me a drink, and I get the urge to lean over and slap him. I'm only in my late twenties, I'm not fucking old. The guys are a little older, all early thirties, but that comment was still unnecessary.

"Whoa, Glory, your eyes are red." Callen slides the drink over to me and steps back a bit. "What's going on? That's not normal."

I take a large gulp of my drink before putting it back down. "Yup, I've heard that a couple of times today. I have no idea. Apparently I may be channeling a little of Nolan's wrath demon."

"But that doesn't happen. A mate doesn't take on another mate's traits," he argues.

"I know. I guess I'm special. It's probably a good thing we're going to Hell tomorrow, because I might have to find a demon doctor and get a checkup. I mean, who the hell has six mates anyway?" I shove my hand out so he can see the rainbow of circles around my demon designation.

He gapes in shock. "Not just six mates, but one from every designation except sloth," he points out helpfully.

"Yeah, what do you think the chances are that's going to change?" I say dryly before slurping down the rest of my cocktail. I need to get moving. Sitting here and drinking isn't helping my nerves or agitation. I need to find Temple and Mason and hope they can fuck it all out of me, because I feel like a junky jonesing for her next fix, or I'm going to bitch slap the next person who looks at me sideways just for the fun of it.

"I have to go. I'll talk to you later," I tell him and then head in the direction of the private rooms.

"Where are you going? Should I call one of the guys?" He follows me down the bar, and a worried line forms between his eyebrows.

"Meeting two of my new mates in room five," I tell him, delighting in watching his worry turn to disgust.

He stops following me and abruptly turns around, muttering, "Didn't think this through when I agreed to work here. Can't wait until the next bounty course."

That makes me giggle a little, but it doesn't last long. Mason and Temple are lucky they are in a private room, otherwise things might have gone pear-shaped if I'd found them giving everyone a show. I get to door five, and the red light above the door is lit, showing the room is occupied, but I knock anyway. They are expecting me, so I'm not concerned that I'm going to interrupt anything. I only hope this isn't going to be awkward.

Chapter Five

The door opens, and Mason appears, his eyes smoldering with desire as his lips turn up in a small smirk. "You came. Theodore and I were just discussing whether or not you would be brave enough. He was worried you would think it was too soon, but I knew you'd want to come." He says that so suggestively, I feel my wrath morphing to desire as my body starts to burn with need, but then I think about what he said.

"Theodore?"

He steps away from the doorway and gestures for me to enter. "You didn't think Temple was his real name, did you?" he asks, and I shrug.

"Yeah, kind of. It's cool."

"Nothing but the moniker bestowed on him by a bunch of degenerates. No, his real name has so much more class, but to be honest, I call him Teddy, because he's so snuggly and sweet when obeying my every desire." Mason's voice is as smooth as velvet, and it trips every kink button I have. I can't wait to obey.

He closes the door behind me, and I come to a

complete stop. Temple… Teddy, which I also love, is in the middle of the room, completely naked and wrapped in red rope like Mason has gift wrapped him for me. His large cock stands at attention, accentuated by the rope wrapped around the base of it, lifting it and his balls higher. His eyes were closed, but he opens them and stares at me with unfettered lust and no small amount of insecurity. I hate seeing the insecurity in his gaze and vow to fix it immediately.

"Whoa, look at my pretty present." I clap my hands. "You've wrapped him so nicely for me." I lean in and give Mason a quick kiss on the lips, but he's quicker than I am, and he sweeps me up into his arms and kisses me hard. He doesn't wait for me to comply, forcing his tongue between my lips and plundering my mouth, taking what he wants without remorse. I melt into his arms. I do love feeling wanted, and there's no hiding his own erection behind his tight black boxers.

When he pulls away, I'm breathless and panting with need, my core aching. "Whoa," I mutter, pressing a finger to my lips, and he just gives me that maddening smirk.

"When we're in this room, I'm in charge, and good boys and girls get rewarded, okay?" Mason says, not allowing me to move away from him.

I give him my own smirk. "Yes, sir."

His eyes crinkle as his smirk turns into a full-blown smile. "Ah, Glory, you're going to be my favorite type of brat, but today is about rewarding our brave and courageous Teddy. He stepped out into open fire to protect our family, and he needs to be rewarded for that, don't you think?" He steps back and allows us to turn and look at our beautifully gift wrapped Teddy.

Mason's skills at shibari are amazing. His ropes wrap around Teddy in such a beautifully artistic way and are just tight enough to bring a flush to the pale man's skin.

"I would love to reward him for his bravery," I tell Mason, my mouth watering.

"How about we lay him down on the bed so both of you will be more comfortable?" Mason steps away from me and over to our mate. His thighs are wrapped, but his legs are not bound in place, so with Mason's arm on his, Teddy obediently follows behind him as they move to the bed. He helps him lie down because his arms are bound across his chest. I also follow behind, but before I can climb up on the bed, Mason stops me.

"Get naked, Glory. I think Teddy also deserves to have a pretty sight, don't you?"

I quickly strip off my shirt before unzipping my pants, shimmying out of them until I'm standing in my functional sports underwear. There's nothing sexy about them, but they are comfortable while chasing bad guys. Still, I can see that neither of them are upset about the lack of lingerie.

"Look at all the beautiful creamy skin, Teddy." Mason steps behind me, running his hands over my body. "It's going to flush beautifully after I use my tools on it." His words caress my ear, and I let my head drop back against his shoulder as he draws down the zipper on the front of my sports bra, letting it fall open as he massages my breasts, pushing them together and up in display for Teddy.

"Don't you wish you could get your mouth on these?" he asks his captive audience, who watches with wide-eyed awe and no small amount of desire. Teddy nods, but Mason tuts.

"Words, Teddy, we want your words."

"She's gorgeous," he mutters roughly, and I preen. "I want to get those pretty tits into my mouth so badly."

"Doesn't he obey so nicely? And he's not wrong," Mason says, dropping his hand away from my tits and sliding the edges of my undies down. He doesn't stop, just hooks his fingers in them and pushes them down my legs, leaving me naked. I shake my bra down my arms and let it drop to the floor as well.

Instead of standing up, though, Mason pushes my legs a little wider and leans in, burying his face between my legs. My knees buckle as he slides his tongue through my folds, but his big hands circle my thighs, keeping me upright. The moan that slips from my mouth is loud.

"Fuck. Oh shit, that feels good." I tilt my hips slightly, giving him better access. Need pounds through my body, and I ache to be filled, but before long, he pulls away.

He stands up, running his tongue across his lips. "Fuck, Teddy, she's sweet and juicy. You should taste her." He looks slightly unhinged, his eyes wide. He moves to the side of the bed and leans down, and I watch as he kisses Teddy, letting him lick his lips. He smirks as he pulls away, and Teddy tries to chase him with his mouth. "But let's give him his reward first, and then we will make sure your every desire is taken care of, I promise," he tells me, gesturing for me to climb up onto the bed.

I don't hesitate. I'm starving, and filling my belly with Teddy's cum is exactly what I want right now. It would be better if it was both of them, but I'm not in charge… this time.

I crawl up the bed and situate my body between his spread legs. I don't hesitate to wrap my lips around Teddy's cock. It's a bit of a stretch, but using my tongue and some spit, I lube it until it can slide in and out of my mouth easily and wrap my hand around the base for extra stimulation. I have no gag reflex, so soon enough, my nose touches his pelvis, and he's panting and wriggling, his thighs flexing beneath me. Mason has moved around behind me and climbed up onto the bed.

"Fuck, you look sexy with Teddy's cock down your throat. Normally, I'd tease you a little… or a lot, but you've had a long ass day. Finding yourself with three more mates can't be easy," he says, his hands caressing my body. "And you've handled it like a champion. Teddy and I are so lucky to have such a kind, competent, and beautiful mate. Aren't we, Teddy?"

Teddy mutters something, but Mason runs a finger through my dripping folds, and I get distracted, my eyes rolling back in my head as he circles a finger around my oversensitive clit. I was ready the moment I walked into the room and saw the setup. I'm desperately horny, and only these two can fix it.

Mason pulls away as I continue to suck on Teddy's cock. I feel more than see him get undressed, and as much as I want to take a peek at his naked form, I don't want to get in trouble and be denied what I'm desperately craving. There will be plenty of time for disobeying.

I feel him climb back on the bed and thread his fingers through my hair, dragging my mouth off Teddy's dick. "As much as I like seeing you choke on Teddy's cock, I also want to see you ride his face. Teddy, scoot down a little," Mason demands, and Teddy wriggles his whole body like a worm and slides down the bed. I giggle, and he rolls his eyes and smiles sheepishly but doesn't say anything.

"Such a good boy. Now, I want you to straddle his face and lean forward," he instructs me. "Smother him. I want him to choke on your juices."

I'm a little worried, but Teddy gives me a small nod, assuring me, so I do as Mason instructs, but not before I get a stinging slap to my ass cheek.

"Don't think I didn't see that," he chastises me. "I'll let you get away with it this time because our dynamic is new, and you were checking on Teddy's comfort. I appreciate that, but next time, I will punish you if you hesitate."

I settle down over Teddy. His crossed arms make it a little difficult, and I have to lean my weight forward and hold onto the headboard.

I lower down, and a guttural groan leaves my mouth as Teddy's fat tongue lashes out and flicks across my clit before he engulfs my whole pussy in his mouth. It's like he's French kissing it, and holy fuck does it feel good. My hands tighten on the headboard as I struggle not to grind down on his face. My head falls forward, and my eyes drift closed, as I let the pleasure consume me.

"Perfect," Mason murmurs and climbs up on the bed so he's standing next to me. He tangles his hand in my hair and lifts my head, turning me to face him, and then taps my cheek with one finger.

"Open up, princess, I want to feel you choke on my cock now."

I do as he asks, but it's super hard to concentrate on giving good head while my pussy is being plundered by Teddy. Eventually, I give up, and he just uses me, thrusting back and forth into my mouth. When he stops and holds me there, he orders me to swallow.

"Fuck," he growls as my throat constricts around his length. "That feels fucking amazing, but I don't want to come like this." He pulls away and releases my head, going behind me and straddling Teddy as well. The poor man is being smothered by us, but when I look down, his eyes are rolled back in ecstasy.

"Lift up and slide back a little," Mason orders, and I do as I'm told. Teddy's tongue focuses on my clit as Mason slowly slides his wet cock into my aching channel. Our groans are dirty and deep.

"Oh fuck. Teddy, you should feel how hot and tight she is." Mason sounds giddy with pleasure as he thrusts in and out a few times. He moves slowly, and all I really want is for him to fuck me like he means it.

"Actually, you can feel her, Teddy." Mason pulls out suddenly and yanks my hips, dragging me down Teddy's body in a mess of limbs. "Ride our mate, Glory," he orders, and this time, I don't hesitate. I can't wait to feel Teddy's fat cock in my pussy. It's going to stretch it so nicely. I slowly lower myself down, gasping at how good he feels.

"Lean forward, baby," Mason says, and my nipples pucker tighter with the endearment. I love hearing him call me that. Then I feel him line himself up and slide in behind Teddy.

"I don't think that's going to fit," I say, and he chuckles.

"Of course it will. Now, give our mate a kiss to help yourself relax." He pushes down on my head, and I kiss Teddy, tasting myself on his tongue, but he soon distracts me with his mad kissing skills. Shit, this feels as good as what he did to my pussy. Maybe it's the knowledge that he was doing exactly this to my pussy not five minutes ago that makes it so dirty.

"Oh yeah, Teddy, she likes that. She just got wetter," Mason says as he slides a little farther in as my body relaxes into the sensation of being double stuffed. At this angle, my clit rubs along the rope wrapped around the base of Teddy's cock, giving it a delightful amount of friction.

"Okay, Teddy, you stay still, and I'll drive." Mason chuckles and starts to slide in and out, getting deeper each time. He lubed up his cock, and he slides easily along Teddy's dick, and we both groan.

"Not going to last," Teddy mutters, and I rest my head in the crook of his neck, absently nibbling on his skin as my two new mates fuck me stupid, unable to do anything but enjoy it.

Mason picks up the pace, and tingles shoot through all my extremities as I reach the edge and tumble over. I scream loudly and hear Teddy shout as his hips jerk a couple of times, filling me with his cum. Our mad maestro just chuckles and slaps my ass.

"Oh yeah, you're so fucking tight, hot, and wet, filled with Teddy's cum." He suddenly stills and groans, adding his own load to the mess that is my pussy.

Both bonds solidify, and a feeling of rightness flows over me as Mason collapses on top of us, turning me into a Glory sandwich. I just smile because I couldn't think of a better place to be at the moment.

When we wake the next morning, I'm comfortable and warm between my two new guys who are still sleeping soundly. After we sealed our bond a couple of times, we cleaned up using the attached bathroom and headed back upstairs to the apartment. Turns out Carter had made it so Mason's membership card could access the private elevator as well.

Louis left a note on the bench saying there was pizza in the fridge, so the three of us sat around and ate warmed up pizza and got to know each other a little better. It's all well and good for our bodies to be compatible, but I wanted to know their minds. Mason is witty and irreverent, but deep down, there's an intelligent man who is desperate to be part of a family. He just likes to hide it behind suggestive remarks and innuendo.

Teddy is exactly how he looks—strong, steady, and serious—and I think it's going to take a little while for him to relax around us. He's spent so much of his life on edge, he's going to have to retrain himself not to jump or flinch at the slightest movement. It actually makes me want to hug him and not let go.

Right this moment, though, if I don't get more food in my belly, I'm likely to cut the first person who looks at me the wrong way, so I squeeze my body out from between the two large men. Teddy doesn't move, but Mason grumbles and rolls over, throwing his whole body around Teddy. He just grumbles and adjusts his arms to hold Mason. It is the cutest fucking thing, and I quietly reach for my phone on the bedside table and snap a couple of pictures.

Leaving them to rest, because who knows when we'll get a chance to again, I wander to the kitchen. The rooms must be soundproofed, because there is a whole pancake party going on out here, and I didn't hear any of it. The radio is playing, and the girls are dancing, their bodies moving with enthusiasm to a Taylor Swift song on the radio. Louis is at the stove, flipping pancakes, his own booty shaking in time to Taylor, with Nolan and Carter sitting at the kitchen island, coffee mugs in front of them as they speak quietly to each other.

Zoe catches sight of me. "Mom!" She hurries over, grabbing my hand and dragging me back to the chaos. "Dance with us," she commands, so of course I do her bidding. I'm braless and just wearing a men's shirt over a pair of panties, but nobody seems to care as all three men's eyes lock onto me like laser sights while I dance with my two girls until the end of the song.

"Phew, that was fun, but I'm going to need some food if we're going to do that again," I tell both girls, kissing their cheeks before sitting down at the island with Nolan and Carter.

"Girls, go take a seat at the table, your pancakes are ready," Louis calls, and the girls whoop and hurry over to the dining table where there is a variety of toppings and two plates for the little cherubs.

"Wow, what a spread," I say as they take large gulps from their glasses of milk.

"Louis is trying to keep them distracted. Both of them ended up in bed with us last night." Carter cracks his neck to one side and winces. "I woke with Zoe's foot firmly wedged into my back."

"And Zoe had her arms wrapped around my neck so hard, I woke up thinking I was being choked out." Nolan runs a hand through his hair, biting his lip with worry. "The shooting yesterday really messed with them. They were finally starting to sleep through the night again after the kidnapping."

"Poor babies. Let's eat and get this show on the road. Hopefully we'll find somewhere safer for them to be in Hell."

"I spoke to my parents. I'm going to leave the girls with them. I don't want them caught in any cross fire that might be aimed at you again, and it gives us time to sort everything out without having to worry about them," Nolan explains, and my stomach sinks with guilt.

"I'm so sorry," I start, and he shakes his head, reaching for my hand.

"Don't be stupid. This isn't your fault, it's all Bridgette's. She tried to kidnap them to start with, and then she wanted to kill you, and now she took the hit out on you. The damn woman has lost her fucking mind."

Before I can answer, Teddy appears in the corridor. His hair is all over the place, and he still looks half asleep. We all watch in amused silence as he stumbles into the living area, squinting against the brightness. He absently kisses me on the head before beelining to the coffee machine and pouring himself a cup. He doesn't add anything to it, just drinks it straight black, and then he sighs with relief after he finishes half a cup.

Zoe's giggle breaks the silence as she points to Teddy. "You look like you've been pulled backwards through a thistle bush," she tells him, miming his hair sticking out at all angles, copying words she must have heard from my mother.

He blushes and pats his hair, trying to make it behave. "I went to bed with wet hair, and it doesn't like it when that happens," he explains.

"Don't worry about it. Come and have breakfast." Louis points at one of the chairs at the table. "You too, Glory. You need your energy after such a trying couple of days."

The two of us do as he says and help ourselves to the mound of food. Aria jumps up and disappears toward the bedrooms.

"Whoa, slow down, rug rat. Where are you off to in such a hurry?" We don't hear her answer, but Mason is smiling when he joins us. He looks a little more put together than Teddy. He's fully dressed in his clothes from yesterday, and his hair has been brushed. When he leans down to brush a kiss across my lips, I can taste that he's brushed his teeth as well.

"Morning, gorgeous," he says, smirking his

trademark smirk before kissing Teddy too. Zoe's mouth drops open in surprise, and I wince. Shit. I'm not sure how we are going to deal with this. She frowns, and I wait for the fallout.

"I want a good morning kiss too," she grumbles, sticking her lip out and pouting. Both Mason and I blink with surprise before he graces her with a blinding smile.

"Oh, my darling Zoe, how could I ever forget you? Will you ever forgive me?" He dramatizes putting his hand against his chest before hurrying around to her side of the table and snatching her out of her chair, whirling her around, then smothering her little face with kisses.

She giggles madly as he smacks his own lips together. "Hmm, maple syrup kisses. Delicious." He places her back in her chair before taking the one on the other side of her.

I'm still blinking with surprise when Aria returns to the table with a brush clasped in her hand. She slowly approaches Teddy.

"If you want, I can brush it for you," she offers shyly, holding out her brush.

Oh my goodness. I feel tears prickle my eyes. Despite how rough yesterday was, it seems like maybe our family is going to be okay. I watch as Teddy practically melts in his chair, a soft smile gracing his face.

"Thank you, that would be lovely," he tells the girl, who smiles like he made her whole day.

"How about you let him finish breakfast first, and then you can go over to the couch and do it?" Nolan jumps up and grabs the brush out of his daughter's hand, guiding her back to the table. He helps her into her chair, and when her back is to him, I see him mouth, "Thank you," to our new mate, who blushes and drops his head to look at his lap.

Mason chuckles next to me, shoving a mouthful of pancakes into his mouth. Looks like he's happy with everything too.

"Well, it seems like last night was successful," Carter gloats as Nolan puts the brush on the couch for Temple and Aria when they finish eating.

The girls are happily chatting when the doorbell rings. Someone trying to enter the apartment from the ground floor can ring the bell, and we can send the elevator to retrieve them.

"Who could that be?" I still haven't had a chance to start my plate of pancakes. Max is missing, so I assume Kade retrieved him when he finished his shift. "Nobody else knows we're here." My heart starts to race as Carter gets up and crosses over to the elevator, using the security panel to see who is downstairs. Maybe it's my mom, because it doesn't take him long before he sends the elevator to retrieve them.

I can tell by the look on his face, though, that it's not when he turns around. "Glory, I know he upset you yesterday, but I think we should hear him out and get to the bottom of everyone's feelings so we can make an informed decision. That way, when we go to Hell, we have the right information if we need to partition Lucifer."

I know exactly who it is once Carter says all of that, and my worry turns to annoyance. Ben is the last person I want to deal with this morning, but Carter isn't wrong. First, though, I need a decent meal to deal with whatever crap Ben is going to bring to the day.

Chapter Six

Ben steps hesitantly into the apartment looking around with wide-eyed awe. I'm not sure if it's an act or if he really is impressed.

"Come on in. Do you want some breakfast?" Louis calls, getting up and heading back to the stove to turn on the pan again. He knows we haven't even cracked the surface of our hunger, and he starts to pour in more pancake batter.

"Coffee?" Nolan offers, going over and grabbing a cup out of the cupboard.

Ben nods, still not saying a word, and I don't feel the need to break the silence either. He made his feelings fairly fucking clear yesterday when he left without a goodbye.

He takes the cup Nolan passes him and looks around awkwardly, taking in Mason and then Teddy, his eyes widening slightly at his lack of clothes.

Shaking his head, he turns to me. "I want to apologize for how I reacted yesterday. I wasn't expecting to meet my mate—now or ever, really—and it was a huge shock. I know I handled it badly, and I probably hurt you." His gaze doesn't settle on me, flittering between all of us like he doesn't want to meet anyone's gaze. It's shifty as shit, and I have no desire to accept his apology.

"Girls, why don't you take your plates and have a picnic in bed? I'll turn the TV on in our room, and you can watch cartoons in there," Nolan suggests. Thankfully, the girls are easily distracted once Aria extracts a promise from Teddy to come find her so she can brush his hair when he finishes breakfast.

While he gets them settled, I make introductions. "Ben, this is Carter, Louis, Theo, and Mason." I point to each man in turn. "And Nolan is with the girls. You met them yesterday. He's their father. I'm Glory. We're your mates."

Ben's eyes almost bug out of his head. "All of you? Shit, this is worse than I thought," he mutters and starts to pace back and forth. He's so agitated, I worry his coffee is going to spill onto the floor.

"Hey, easy." Carter holds up his hands in a placating manner. "Why don't you take a seat, and you can tell us what has you so wound up?"

Ben is acting like a trapped, wounded animal. This isn't normal behavior, and despite my pain, I know we need to get to the bottom of the situation.

"Why didn't you ever think you were going to meet your mate?" Teddy asks without judgment as he puts an arm around my shoulders and pulls me into his side. He can obviously tell that I'm hurt and need comfort, and I'm thankful.

"God, things couldn't get much worse, so I may as well tell you." Ben dramatically throws himself onto the sofa as Nolan rejoins us, his eyes widening slightly at his over-the-top behavior. I feel my anger start to rise.

"For fuck's sake, being mated to me isn't the end of the world. I'll have you know that I have mad fucking sex skills, not to mention I'm an excellent cook. I suck at housework, but I make up for it in so many other ways." I can't help the quiver in my voice even though I'm trying for indignation.

"Ah, babe. Don't be upset. The kid obviously doesn't know a good thing when it leaps up and bites him on the dick." Mason winks.

Teddy shakes his head with exasperation. "Seriously?" he asks, and Mason shrugs.

"What? He's obviously `young. Maybe he's a virgin. Are you a virgin? I can assure you, we can ease you into the joys of sex, no problem."

Ben stares at Mason with disbelief, and Carter snorts with amusement. Nolan and Louis just watch with fascination, breakfast completely forgotten, but thankfully he turned off the stove. "So... not the problem."

Ben puts his hand up for Mason, and I worry he's going to flip him off, but instead, he says, "Be quiet now, the adults are talking."

"What a brat," Mason mutters, but I can see a gleam of interest in his eyes.

"Notice he didn't answer though?" Teddy rumbles quietly in my ear. No, he didn't, did he? I wonder exactly how old Ben is, because right this very moment, he doesn't look much older than my brothers.

"Tell us what's going on." Nolan ignores Mason's antics and tries to get the conversation back on track.

"You know how when you leave Hell, you have to have a job lined up or a family business to step into?" Ben asks, and everyone but Teddy and me nods their heads.

"Ah, no." I point to us. "We didn't know that."

Louis sighs. "Sorry, muffin cheeks." He turns to Ben. "Neither Glory nor Theo have been to Hell," he explains, and I love how he uses Theo's real name and not his nickname. "Both of them were born here on Earth."

"When a demon wants to come to Earth, they can't come just for fun, that's when demons get into trouble. They need to have arrangements. A lot of demons like the three of us had a family business that we inherited. When the demon running it wants to return to Hell, someone else from the family usually takes over. Wrathful Bail Bonds was Nolan's parents', the club was my parents', and

Tasty Treats belonged to Louis's family," Carter explains to the two of us.

"But those of us without family to leave us a business or a method of income must arrange a job," Ben explains.

"Like how your mother employs demons to work in her brothel," Carter tells me. "They are all sponsored and have a guaranteed form of cash income, so they don't get on the government's radar."

"Ah, no social security." I catch on, and it seems Temple does too.

"Yes, well, my benefactor wasn't happy to find out that I have a mate," Ben says flatly, and his eyes are dull as his spare hand drums nervously on the arm of the sofa.

"Your benefactor wasn't happy?" Louis sounds as confused as the rest of us. "How is it his business? In fact, he should be more than happy because it releases him from the responsibility of making sure you don't cause problems."

We see Ben swallow nervously. "Yes, well, if my travel to Earth had been approved through the proper channels it might be."

"What do you mean?" Nolan leans forward, resting his elbows on his knees. All of his attention is on Ben.

"You're an illegal," Mason grumbles, "aren't you?"

"An illegal?" Teddy sounds as confused as I am, which is a relief.

"Some demons can't get approval through the proper channels. They have no sponsor or family, like they said originally, and they don't like the employment options available to them. There is a black market that offers Earth time in exchange for servitude. When you said your benefactor, you actually meant *the* benefactor, a shady asshole who traffics demons." Mason's voice has gone hard, a change from the joking tone from before.

"Yes. He is very powerful. When you make a deal, he uses blood magic to bind you to him." Ben pulls down the neck of his shirt and shows us a brand-like mark on his chest. It's a stylized M. "It allows him to track me, and it's how he knew I had found my mate. He could feel it through the brand. He likes collecting pretty things and doesn't like to share. He's a very jealous demon."

"You're his boyfriend?" I ask, suddenly feeling queasy.

Ben shrugs. "I have no special talents or skills, nor a rich family, and I wanted to come to Earth. He owns the club I performed in last night. He allows me to do what I want as long as I appear on his arm and fulfill his needs. It's an easy job. He's a handsome man, and he has many at his beck and call. I'm not required more than once a week."

"So you would like to stay with this man? You

would like me to petition Lucifer to erase our mating?" I'm heartbroken that he wants to stay with this predator over being mated to me. I feel nauseous.

Ben shudders and shakes his head vehemently. "God, no. I can't stand him. It was fun at first, but I have come to see that he is truly evil. He's obsessed with blood magic and a magic book full of nasty spells—binding spells, tracking spells, spells that trap souls…" This is all starting to sound a little familiar. "And demons aren't the only ones he deals with. He's recently been dealing with humans, promising to grant their wishes in exchange for their souls."

"Holy fuck, he's becoming the embodiment of Satan," I whisper, and Ben nods, blushing.

"While we're giving full disclosure, it's my fault you were shot at last night. When he questioned me using his spells, I had to tell him who my mate was. I'm ashamed to admit that he forced me to come to your place yesterday. He has a human in his thrall —Bridgette."

Well, I guess that answers the question of where Bridgette is.

"She wants you dead. The gunman followed me and opened fire, but I wasn't prepared to stand there and let him kill you, so I tackled you. The brand on my chest is supposed to instill complete obedience, but I think the mating bond is overriding it, and I can disobey. That's how I've been able to tell you all this. Please help me, Glory. I don't want to be bound to this demon anymore. I want to be your mate, but I don't know how to get out of this without endangering all of you," he pleads, his focus finally on me, and I see tears in his eyes. He is either a very good actor, or he is scared out of his wits.

A wave of relief washes over me. Despite everything, I like Ben. I was so sad when I thought he didn't want to be with me because, yes, I'm gluttonous, so I make the decision to do whatever I can to get him out of a bad situation. I can tell from the look on all my mates' faces that they feel the same way—all except one. Throughout the story, I watched out of the corner of my eye as Mason became more and more tense.

I need us all to be on the same page here, so I ask, "Mason, what's wrong?"

"What is your benefactor's name?" His fists are clenched, and I can see he's grinding his teeth.

"Mabuz," Ben announces, and we all tense up.

"Is that the same Mabuz who scammed the book from my mom and entrapped your ex?" I ask, and Mason nods stiffly. It's obvious he's trying to hold his shit in.

"Yes, he's always gloating about how he managed to steal the book right out from under

Lucifer's nose." Ben sighs heavily, and I get the feeling that more bad news is coming.

"Just spit it out, Ben. We may as well know everything. We don't need surprises on this trip to Hell." I'm getting annoyed now as Teddy gets up and goes around to give Mason some comfort. He's rigid with anger and glaring at Ben like he's somehow responsible, but he was just as duped as everyone else. In fact, he may be the next soul in a Fabergé egg if he isn't careful.

"Mabuz has big plans. He wants to rule Hell. He thought his book of blood magic would be the key to that, but so far, he hasn't had any success. He knows he can't break Lucifer's bond to Hell because it's the land itself that created that bond, but the Hell heir has no such bond. He thinks if he can take out the Hell heir, then the land will accept him as the next ruler of Hell. It would be a challenge much like mate challenges." Ben's words have everyone's eyes widening with alarm.

"Fuck." My gaze swings to Carter and Nolan. "My mom can definitely not go to Hell."

"I'll call your dads and let them know." Nolan pulls out his cell and disappears toward the office in the back.

"We need to stop this demon." Carter sounds pissed. "Why hasn't Lucifer done anything about him?"

"It's why Mabuz sticks mainly to Earth. Lucifer

has no jurisdiction here. He can send his bounty hunters to retrieve demons, but there has to be proof of his crimes, and up until now, he hasn't had any proof. Lucifer himself can't actually leave Hell. Both he and the land would suffer, not to mention Mabuz with his book of magic has tricks up his sleeve no normal demon would be able to defeat." Ben sounds resigned.

Mason's glare turns into an evil grin of satisfaction. "Well, isn't it lucky that I actually have proof now? Mabuz is going to suffer tenfold for what he's done to other people." He must be talking about the Fabergé egg he stole that his ex's soul is trapped inside.

"Yeah, but Lucifer still can't leave Hell," I point out. "How are we going to stop Mabuz with that spell book? And now I'm worried about my mom." I have a sudden change of heart. "Maybe she does need to go to Hell. She's in more danger from Mabuz on Earth. Why do you think he hasn't tried to kill her yet?"

"Mabuz doesn't know that she's the Hell heir for sure. He suspects it, but when they were together, she didn't have the mark on her. If he kills her without being sure, then that will definitely catch Lucifer's attention," Ben explains.

"How do you have all this information?" Mason asks suspiciously, and Ben shrugs.

"I pay attention, and Mabuz tends to forget

other people are around when he's scheming and does that evil villain thing where he monologues his plan out loud. It's ridiculous, but I've learned a lot."

Nolan returns, and he's frowning. "Your mom claims she's not the official heir. She said in theory, maybe, but last time she was in Hell, the land hadn't marked her. She thinks it's because she's not worthy after she betrayed Lucifer and gave Mabuz the book."

"So Hell has no heir. That's even worse. It means that Mabuz could waltz in there and claim it. He can't find out." Ben is twitchy and agitated. "I can't go back there, but I can't resist the summons once he calls me. My mark doesn't stop burning until I'm in his presence."

"Will his influence be able to reach you in Hell?" Teddy asks, and Ben shrugs again.

"I have no idea."

I stand up and gather the plates. "We can eat when we get to Hell. Let's get moving. I, for one, don't want to stand around and wait for Mabuz to summon Ben. What about the rest of you?"

"I agree. I'll go get the girls dressed." Nolan turns but then stops. "Come on, Theo, you need your hair brushed." He chuckles, and Teddy blushes, but after checking that Mason is okay, he follows Nolan without question.

Louis is placing the things I pass him into the dishwasher when the doorbell rings. Ben jumps up, looking panicked, and Carter goes over to the security screen. He sends the elevator down without hesitation, so I know it's not anyone to worry about.

"Who is it?" Ben asks, wringing his hands together.

"Relax," Carter tells him. "It's just Glory's friend Kerry."

"Kerry? What is she doing here?" I put my hands on my hips and arch an eyebrow at my mate. He's smirking.

"Kerry is going to help us get into Hell undetected by Lucifer. We don't want him to know we're there straightaway. We need to gauge how he feels about his absent niece before we ask for his help or whatever the plan seems to be. It changes by the minute." Carter sounds frustrated. I know he and Nolan both like to have plans, and all of this happened so quickly we haven't really had time to form a solid one yet. I think getting the girls to safety is the first priority, and then we can finally take a breath and make one.

I can't deny it will be nice to have some backup in the form of Kerry, and her dad is Lucifer's head bounty hunter, so if she doesn't know her way around Hell and its politics, then no one does.

Chapter Seven

Kerry has us drive to a nearby Walmart, where we all get out. The guys grab the bags we brought with us, and we leave the cars parked in the lot.

"What about the cars?" I ask, looking back at them, worried they won't be here when we get back.

"They'll be fine. A couple of the guys are going to come get them and take them back to Wrathful Bail Bonds. I'll just let them know when we return, and they will bring them back." Carter throws his spare arm around my shoulders and gives me a side hug, and I kind of just slump into it. I'm feeling all kinds of things at the moment, like confusion and anxiety, but mostly I'm nervous, and this helps.

"Don't they think it's weird?" I haven't met many of their actual bond agents, just the two who were with us during the drag queen takedown. The rest are usually out on jobs.

"We have a couple of demons working for us, so they know the deal," Nolan says, looking around the parking lot carefully like he's expecting an attack at any moment.

The girls are chatting excitedly with Kerry, who is doing a marvelous job of distracting them. Teddy's hair is tied back against his neck with a pretty pink hair tie that I know came from Aria's collection. What a sweetheart to leave it there.

"Aren't we going to get some funny looks when we walk in carrying bags and things?" I'm nervous, so I can't stop asking questions, but we stop, and the bags suddenly disappear from the guys' hands. "Whoa, that's cool." I blink a couple of times to make sure I'm not seeing things. "Did you just put them into an inter-dimensional cubby?" I ask, unable to hide the excitement in my voice. "Mom never taught us to do that."

"Yup, and it means once we get to Hell, we can retrieve them. We can't actually conjure stuff between the Hell plane and Earth, which is why these dimensional hidey-holes come in handy," Nolan explains.

"I'll teach you how to do it if you want." Mason has been mostly quiet this whole time, and he hasn't let Ben out of his sight. I don't think he trusts him one bit, and that's probably not a bad thing. Until we can get that brand removed from his chest, he will be a liability.

"Can Mabuz track you to Hell?" I ask him, and he chews on his lip nervously before nodding.

"I'm not sure, but I think so."

Kerry hears our conversation and asks Louis to swap places with her. He gladly takes the girls' hands now that his are free of bags, and they walk into Walmart. "We'll meet you at the portal in ten," he promises. "We're going to find some things for the girls to take, maybe a new coloring book or something."

"Show me the brand," Kerry demands, putting her hands on her hips. We filled her in on the whole story during the drive over.

Ben pulls the neck of his shirt down, exposing the brand over his left pec. It's bright red and kind of angry looking, but there is no mistaking the large M.

Kerry studies it, her brows furrowed before she looks up and winces. "I've never seen anything like it before. Lucifer can put tracking marks on prisoners, but they look nothing like this, and I know they don't involve blood magic. Dad says it has something to do with the power the land bestowed upon Lucifer. When it's on the prisoner, he can sense where they are in Hell, but they are a symbol, not a letter, and they are black, similar to the demon designation mark."

"So we don't know if Mabuz can track him to Hell or not? Great, we're kind of screwed. How long do you think it will be before Mabuz summons you?" I ask him, and he seems to shrink in on himself, but is it real fear?

"I guess it depends on if he can track me or not. If he can, and he realizes I've left Earth, then it will be immediately. We aren't allowed to return to Hell without permission, especially because if we go the normal way, then they will know that I don't have permission to leave, and that brings his venture to the attention of the authorities. If he can't track me, then probably a few days. He was plotting when I left after his failed attempt to kill Glory. He still needs to fill his half of the bargain with Bridgette before he gets her soul. He uses human souls to make his magic more powerful."

"Great, so the sooner we can get Glory to Hell, the better. Let's not stand around then." Teddy seems edgy and just as cautious as Nolan had been.

"Hang on! How did Mabuz get you out of Hell if you don't go the normal way?" Kerry asks Ben.

"His book of blood magic allows him to make a portal, but it takes a toll and a lot of blood, so he doesn't allow it very often. Maybe once or twice a year."

"I vote we leave him here," Mason growls menacingly, but Ben doesn't even blink. He doesn't seem to be scared of Mason at all. I wonder if it's because he knows they are mates or if Mabuz is just so scary that nothing else fazes him.

"Can you tell him you're visiting your family?" Kerry asks him, and he shakes his head.

"I don't have any. My parents both died when I was younger, and I don't have any siblings. The reason I wanted to go to Earth was because I aged out of foster care."

"Oh my god! How old are you?" I ask, horrified. Am I committing a crime by having him mated to me?

He chuckles, and it's the first sign of a smile I've seen since I met him that first day. "Relax, Glory, I'm twenty-two. I've been on Earth for four years."

He's still a few years younger than me but not completely in the illegal zone. I heave out a sigh of relief, but Carter has reached the limit of his patience. "Can we go? We can discuss everything else once we get settled in a hotel."

"A hotel?" Kerry screeches loudly. "You will do no such thing. Our family home is empty since my parents live in Lucifer's palace, so you can go there. It will be harder for anyone to find you because there will be no record of a stay or monetary transaction."

"Actually, that will be great. Your parents' place is big enough for all of us to fit comfortably. Thank you." Nolan gives her a quick hug and a kiss on the cheek.

I keep forgetting they are old family friends. I wonder if he and Kerry ever had a thing. If he was one of my brothers' best friends, I would have always been hanging around, but she quickly shoots that down.

"Eww, I know where those lips have been." She pushes him away, gagging.

"Hey," I complain, and she winces.

"Sorry, I don't mean you. I just know what he was like when we were teenagers. Can you say man-whore with a capital M?"

"Yeah, I don't doubt it. I'm pretty sure all three of them were."

Carter runs a sheepish hand through his hair as I give him the evil eye. "Hey, I'm a lust demon. I have needs. Again, though, let's move inside and get this show on the road. If you want to fight about this later, I can give you my full attention when we are safe." He opens his arms and shepherds us inside, not letting anyone else talk.

It's early morning, and the store seems to be full of child-free moms because they just dropped them off at school. The thirsty moms eye my men like they are the finest piece of steak on special in the meat aisle. I have to glare at bold ones twice when they redirect their shopping carts a little too close to one of the guys to brush against them.

"Hey, girl, rein it in," Kerry mutters, jabbing an elbow into my side. "You're starting to growl." She gapes at me when I meet her eyes. "Holy shit, Glory, your eyes are changing colors like a freaking rainbow. Red, yellow, and violet. That's wrath, greed, and pride. What the hell is going on? That isn't normal."

"Well, I have six mates, one for each sin except sloth, and that's not normal either. Nothing about what's happening is normal. I have a hit out on me, and the psycho bitch doesn't care if her kids are taken out in the cross fire, which definitely isn't fucking normal. None of this is normal!" I retort, unable to hide the growing hysteria in my voice. We get a few looks, and the women who had been eyeing my mates turn their carts and hurry away in the opposite direction. At least they have some sense of self-preservation.

"Deep breaths, Glory. Bursting into flames here won't go over well." Teddy takes my hand and squeezes it, lifting my chin so I can look at him. "Breathe deeply, in and out."

"Okay, right this way." Kerry turns on her heel and picks up the pace, leading us straight to the changing rooms. Louis and the girls are already there.

"Come on, we need to be quick, because we're going to get funny looks if we're not." She pushes open the door of the one that says, "Out of order," and flicks a switch on the wall.

"What does that do?" I ask her, but it's Mason who answers.

"That's to distort the cameras so they don't see

us go in and not come back out. A big group of us will draw attention. If there was an attendant here, we would go one or two at a time, but time is of the essence, and there isn't an attendant here."

"Is there ever? I don't think I've ever used the changing rooms at Walmart before." I glance around, and there seems to be a distinct lack of customer service people.

Kerry shrugs, not looking worried. "Sometimes, but not often. I've never run into any problems. Okay, I'll go first, and you guys follow a couple at a time. Remember to pull the door closed between groups, and for the last person through, make sure it's closed behind you."

She opens the door and walks in, closing it behind her. I hear a whoosh, and there's an electric crackle in the air, and then it's gone. When Nolan opens the door, she's not there.

"Come on, girls, you can come with me." He holds out his hands, and the girls step forward. We explained what was going to happen to them, and although they look nervous, there's a skip of excitement in Zoe's step. Aria is certainly more cautious.

"We're going to see our grandparents?" Zoe asks, looking up at her dad, and he nods.

"Yes, they are so excited that you're coming to stay with them."

The girls haven't been to Hell yet. Originally, that would have been hard to explain to Bridgette.

I'm almost certain she knows they are demons, but it was easier for Nolan's parents to come to Earth. They need permission to visit, however, and it can only be once or twice a year for three days at a time. Those are the rules. It would have been different if they stayed involved with Wrathful Bail Bonds, because then they would be allowed to come and go as they please, but they handed it over to Nolan. Eventually, Nolan will do the same, handing it over to my brothers or maybe one of the girls when they are older. I can't see Aria being a bounty hunter, but I bet Zoe would have the right enthusiasm for it. I guess we will have to wait and see, or maybe we'll stay on Earth and run it. Who knows what will happen?

The door closes again, and the portal activates. Carter holds out his hand, gesturing for Mason and Teddy to go. "You guys go next, and the three of us will follow."

Teddy steps forward, but Mason glares at Ben. "You can come with us. I don't want to let you out of my sight."

Ouch, Mason still isn't any closer to trusting Ben. I guess I can't blame him. He has a good reason to hold a grudge against Mabuz, and he sees Ben as an extension of him for now. Hopefully that will eventually change.

Both guys give me a quick kiss, even though it's literally going to be seconds until I see them again. I get all warm and fuzzy and have a stupid grin on my face as the door closes behind them, despite being disappointed that Ben just gave me a nod. Shit, maybe I don't trust him either. He says he wants to be my mate and free of Mabuz, but actions speak louder than words, and he hasn't shown that's how he feels. He avoids looking at me, and he went in the other car instead of riding with me. Teddy and Mason won't let me out of their sight, and the other three were like that during our first few weeks as well.

"I take it last night went well?" Carter asks, looking amused, and I feel my cheeks heat a little.

"You could say that. Teddy and Mason are amazing. I never thought I would need or want anyone except for the three of you, but they just seem to fit right into the family, don't they?"

"Yes, it's almost like it's meant to be," Louis muses thoughtfully.

"Exactly. Are you guys okay with all this?" I haven't really had a chance to talk to them about it.

"I mean, we weren't expecting anyone else to be a part of our mating group, but we're not upset. Mates are fated, so how can we be upset if fate decides you need more than the three of us?" Carter smiles and pulls me in for a hug. "And it doesn't hurt that they are sexy as hell too," he mutters quietly into my ear, and I grin. His hug feels amazing. Louis steps up behind me, and they sandwich me between them. My whole body relaxes. I really needed this.

"I know, right?" I grin as I soak in the comfort they provide. "But what about Ben? Do you think he's telling the truth or is he playing us?"

I feel them both stiffen, and when they pull back, Carter is frowning. I turn my head to look at Louis and see he is too.

"I'm not sure, my little strudel. I think we need to keep a close eye on him though. My gut tells me he's not telling us everything." Louis's accent thickens with his worry.

"No. He doesn't seem to want to get to know you or get too close to you. I'm wondering if he's ever been interested in girls." Carter scratches his beard scruff. "He's obviously interested in guys because he's been Mabuz's companion for four years, but fate wouldn't give you a strictly gay mate, would it? That would be cruel for both of you."

"Ugh, I don't know. Why do I need any more? Maybe we should dissolve the mating as well as his bond with Mabuz, but to do any of that, we have to go see Lucifer, and who knows how well he's going to take seeing his long-lost niece. We have quite a few things to tell him though. He's going to want to know all about Mabuz and what he's up to."

I pull the door open, impatient to get this show on the road. I don't know anything about going to Hell, so I don't know if we'll appear in a populated area or not, and if not, then how do we get around Hell? I wonder if they have cars.

"You know we'll support you in every way. Lucifer is mostly reasonable. I'm sure he will be thrilled to see you, but maybe not so thrilled to hear about Mabuz's scheming," Louis says, stepping into the changing room behind me, followed by Carter who pulls the door closed and flicks the switch on the wall so the cameras go back to normal. "But let's not make hasty decisions about Ben. Get to know him, and maybe have a private conversation asking him what he really wants. He may just be shy."

"Pfft, shy? Did you see him when he was Poppy Cox? I don't think there is a shy bone in his body."

"Maybe he needs the full outfit to be like that, you don't know, just keep an open mind," Carter suggests as the back of the changing room starts to swirl, and we fall silent as I watch in awe as a portal to Hell opens before us. I kind of want to slap them both for being so damn reasonable. Logically, I know why they are, but emotionally, I want them to be as hurt as I am.

"Whoa! How does that happen?" I mutter quietly, not wanting to upset the portal or anything.

"I don't know exactly, but it reads that a demon has entered the booth and activates. If, for some reason, a human stepped in, it wouldn't do anything." Carter is close behind me so all three of us can fit in the booth together. As the portal expands, it sort of shimmers like a mirror. "Okay, let's go." He grabs my hand, and we follow Louis into it. I scrunch my eyes closed and pray to live as I approach. I hear Carter chuckle quietly, but I'm too busy praying not to die to care. My stomach kind of lurches sideways a little, and I feel a little light-headed, but a cool sensation washes over me before a rush of hot air replaces it.

"Open your eyes, Glory," Nolan encourages me, and the two girls giggle.

"Wasn't that fun?" Zoe asks.

I open my eyes, and Zoe is jumping up and down on the spot, but as I look around, I'm too gobsmacked to pay her too much attention. Gone is the very crowded changing cubicle, and in its place is a large, open area that looks like a very cliched hellscape. A wide open, dusty, rocky space stretches before us with what looks like lava cracks in the ground coming from a smoking volcano far in the distance. Craggy ridges dot the landscape without a blade of grass to be seen. The sky is tinged with red, and it's as hot as, well, dare I say hell? I can see something move out on the plain, but it's too far away to make out what it is. I swallow nervously.

Chapter Eight

"Oh my god! This is awful. We can't bring the girls here. They need to go home now." The smell of sulfur is strong despite how far away the volcano is.

A hand grips my shoulder and turns me around. The portal shimmers innocently to one side, but behind it, the scenery changes drastically. Gone is the broken, barren wasteland, and in its place is a paved road with a building to one side. The landscape is green and inviting, and there are trees dotted here and there.

"Lucifer thinks it's funny to have the portal facing Mt. Doom so that when unsuspecting demons or humans arrive, like you and Teddy, you freak out. The rest of us know it's there, so it's kind of pointless," Mason explains.

There is so much for me to unpack with that sentence, I don't know where to start. Humans can come to Hell? "He called the volcano Mt. Doom?" I mutter incredulously.

"Lucifer has a sense of humor, and you get

bored after being in charge for so many years. He changes its name every ten years."

"I know demons are long-lived, but Lucifer seems even more so."

"The rumors are it's because he's tied to the land. I don't know, maybe you could ask him when you meet him. Being his niece may give you some leeway." Mason loses interest in the conversation and moves over to the others.

There seems to be an argument going on, so I also join them, and my mouth drops open in shock. I thought Hell was just another plane similar to Earth, but the talking, three-headed dog who is arguing with Kerry seems to indicate something completely different.

It's dark maroon, almost black in color, and it doesn't seem to be covered in fur. Instead, it seems to have a leather-like hide. Ridges dot his back, and his tail is whip thin with a barb on the end. His heads look a little like a Doberman's but on steroids, and his six lavender eyes shine with intelligence and no small amount of menace.

"Listen, Bussy, can't you just overlook it this time? We really need to stay off Lucifer's radar for the time being. I promise I'll bring you a big buck from Earth next time I come through," Kerry tells the three-headed dog who has a stubborn set to all three of his muzzles.

"Damn it, we forgot about the gatekeeper," Mason mutters. "He's a stickler for rules, and he needs to record all the comings and goings for the official record. Ben is an illegal, and that's never going to fly. We should have remembered to bring a bribe. He's always a difficult asshole."

"Can't we just tell him that Ben was born on Earth like Teddy and me?" I ask him, and he shakes his head.

"No, because all Earth demon births need to be recorded in Hell, and the parent usually sends a notification."

"How will he know? He's just a dog, he can't read or write. I doubt my mother sent a notification when we were born."

"Shhh." Mason claps a hand over my mouth, but it's too late, because three doggy heads turn their attention to me.

"On the contrary, Gloriana Luxure, we have a record of each of Petra Luxure's children." The voice from the head on the left is deep and kind of menacing, and I flinch as his lavender eyes narrow on me. "And we will not turn a blind eye to someone sneaking into Hell."

"Who are you?" I ask, but I'm almost certain I know the answer to this. I'm a fan of Greek mythology.

"We are Cerberus," that same head answers.

"Guardian of the gate and keeper of the realm," the middle head intones in a voice that's slightly sleepy.

"And we are fabulous," the last head speaks with an effeminate lisp, and one of their paws comes up like he's snapping his fingers.

The other two heads glare at him. "Shut it, we've told you not to speak to people."

"You are such bitches." The head huffs and turns so he can't see the other two, his bottom jaw jutting out like he's pouting.

"The illegal must be seized and taken to detainment until we can ascertain how he got to Earth." The left head has refocused on the task at hand and is eyeing Ben like he might make him his next snack.

Kerry stomps her foot. "That's it, Cerberus. I'm done talking with you. You don't control everything around here anymore," Kerry growls, and I flinch. The middle head's eyes flash green before turning back to lavender, and Kerry squeaks in alarm and steps back.

"She is totally going to have her face eaten off," I mutter to no one in particular.

"I want to speak to Julian now. Let him out," Kerry argues, but this gets Nolan's attention.

"Julian?" He looks between Kerry and the dog with wide eyes. "Julian volunteered to be the host?"

Kerry sighs heavily and turns to face us, putting her back to the dog, which I think is stupid, but what would I know? "I'll explain what happened, because some of you are new to Hell. Cerberus was created by the land to guard the portal. He has been Lucifer's constant companion from the start, but for some reason, about three years ago, his body began to break down, despite his soul and mind still being a hundred percent intact. Lucifer consulted the land, who told him he needed to find a host willing to accept Cerberus's soul. It was to be a total sacrifice. Cerberus would assimilate the sacrifice, and they would cease to be. Lucifer was going to use a condemned prisoner, but it needed to be a volunteer. Julian was the only one who volunteered. He was in a dark place. You know how sloth demons can be. Depression is a common side effect, especially those with no outside interests like your brothers, Glory. I think your mother's DNA probably helps counter that too. Julian, though, has never been one hundred percent stable, and he thought if he volunteered, he was at least committing suicide for a noble cause."

Nolan pales considerably at Kerry's words. "He was that depressed? I had no idea." Carter reaches out and gives Nolan's shoulder a squeeze.

"Who is Julian?" I ask, because I have a feeling he's not just somebody they used to know.

"Julian is my brother," Kerry says, which means that, at one stage, he was Nolan's best friend. I eye my mate with concern.

"Yes, after you left Hell, the decline was slow but steady. He lost interest in the family business, and he had no drive or purpose. He did nothing but sit on the couch and sleep. He didn't even stay in contact with any of his other friends. He was in a bad way. Mom and Dad did everything they could, so did Luc, to talk him out of it, but in the end, he made the sacrifice. It was the best thing that could have ever happened to him, though, because instead of being taken completely over, they merged equally, and becoming a part of something gave him drive and purpose for the first time in a long time. Cerberus's arrogance tempered some of the depression too, and when he is in human form, he isn't so sad anymore."

"He's a shifter?" Mason asks, eyeing the dog with interest.

"Kind of. When he is in this form, Julian completely recedes. If Cerberus had his way, he would never allow Julian out, but he has to. He can hold the shift for about a week, but after that, Julian takes over. In the beginning, it was a bitch fight between them, but they came to an agreement to share equal time." Kerry lowers her voice. "When Julian is in charge, Cerberus is completely gone. I'm hoping if I can get Julian here, he will overlook Ben."

"Julian is in agreement, the illegal must be detained." The left head seems to be the one in charge. They obviously heard everything we've been talking about, and why wouldn't they, Cerberus has three sets of ears.

Kerry flinches. "Shit, that isn't good. Let Julian out. I want to hear it in his own voice."

"I'm sorry, Kerry, but Julian actually doesn't want to come out at the moment." It's the right head who answers, his voice holding a hint of sympathy.

"You don't know that," she argues, and the dog seems to shrug his shoulders.

"I'm afraid I do. We have become more in sync with one another over the past couple of months, creating harmony between us. We are more powerful than ever thanks to our symbiotic relation-ship." The three heads turn to look at Nolan. "He is not ready to face you and your lovers. It was rude of you to flaunt them in his face like this." All three heads start to growl at Louis and Carter, who have both moved closer to Nolan at the sign of his distress. Aria whimpers, and Teddy drags her and Zoe behind him though Zoe fights to peek out from behind his legs.

Why is the dog acting so aggressively toward

Nolan if he and Julian were best friends? Then I have an epiphany. I whirl on my mate, propping my hands on my hips. "Holy shit. You weren't just best friends, were you? You were lovers."

Kerry's eyes just about bulge out of her head, and she wrinkles her nose when she looks at Nolan. "Is that right? We always wondered why he was so triggered after you left."

Nolan's cheeks are red, and he won't look her in the eye. "We messed around when we were teenagers. It was nothing serious. You know what demons are like. We're a fairly promiscuous bunch until we find our mates and settle down."

The heads growl louder, and we take a step back. Ben joins the girls behind Teddy with a little squeak. Nolan loses the blush and glares at Cerberus.

"Please, like you were any more faithful to me than I was to you. You tried to convince me we were mates, though you had a revolving door of men and women through our college dorm room. You think I didn't know about that, but you gained quite a reputation around campus. People would talk about Julian Beamus. They said he had connections with Lucifer and must have been blessed by him in the cock department. You couldn't work up much energy for anything else, but you certainly fucked your way through college. Mates don't treat each other like that, which is why I left. I was at least discreet with the other people I had flings with."

Nolan is well and truly pissed by the end of his rant, and Teddy and Ben shuffle the girls farther away, distracting them by asking them to show them what they bought at Walmart. Both girls have a shopping bag clutched in their hands. Louis spoils them.

"Ah, I think we may be getting a little off track here. I'm sure you two have a lot to talk about, but can we please get out of the open? I feel like there is a giant target on our backs." I eye the portal, worried that Mabuz and Bridgette will burst through at any moment.

One of Cerberus's heads lurches out and snaps at me, and before I can stop myself, I find myself slapping his muzzle "Bad dog." I can hear Zoe and Aria crying behind me. Teddy's attempt to distract them didn't work, and they are scared now.

"Oh shit. Now we're fucked. We may as well go back through the portal. My brother may be inside, but their dual instincts are to protect Lucifer and Hell, and you just made an aggressive move," Kerry mutters and takes another step back, followed by my chivalrous mates. I'm on my own, standing up to this beast.

"I don't care. Nobody snaps at my family like that," I state stubbornly.

Cerberus actually yelps and drops to the

ground, cowering. "You smacked us," the right head whimpers.

"You were being unnecessarily aggressive, and you're scaring the little girls. We like to use words, not actions, in our family," I scold calmly though slightly hypocritically.

"Holy fuck, I have never seen Cerberus bow to anyone but Lucifer," Kerry mutters behind me.

"I guess having your brother as a host made him more humble," Mason remarks.

"We were just doing our job," the middle head says mulishly, his eyes blinking sleepily at me.

"And I appreciate that, but I have a feeling personal feelings are clouding your actions," I explain reasonably, and the left head nods.

"Yes, you may be right. We feel so much more now that we are merged with Julian. His feelings when he saw Nolan are complicated, and we don't know how to react."

I crouch down and move closer, giving them all a scratch between the ears.

"It's okay," I coo as they start to make this weird sound, a cross between a purr and a cough. "It can be difficult to regulate our emotions when we feel so much. I find taking a deep breath and pausing helps," I suggest as the beast's tail wags. "And I promise I will make sure I keep Ben in sight the whole time we are in Hell. I know you have a job to do, but would you mind waiting a day or two before you make note of his arrival? I promise I will present us all to Lucifer when we have had time to get settled," I assure the cute puppy who seems to be enjoying the affection I'm bestowing upon them. Poor things are just starved for attention.

"Of course, but I think we will accompany you, just to make sure the illegal doesn't cause any trouble." The left head is eyeing Ben with suspicion.

"Fucking hell, she tamed the beast. Lucifer will be pissed. Who will guard the gate if Cerberus isn't here?" Mason sounds wary, and Kerry shrugs.

"Since he and Julian merged, he doesn't guard the gate full time. He feels when it activates and teleports here to intercept travelers. He appeared here when I arrived."

"Has it really been so long since we were home?" Louis shakes his head. "I can't believe we didn't know any of this."

"I can't believe my parents didn't tell me about Julian," Nolan mutters, still looking at the dog warily. It must be a mind fuck to know a former lover is now a dog. I guess there's a lot to unpack there, but that can wait.

"Okay, where do we go from here?" I stand up after giving each head one last pat.

"My family home is near the palace in the center of the city. We'll go straight there after we drop the girls off." Kerry points down the road, but the city must be far away, because I can't see anything that looks like one anywhere nearby.

"And how does one get around in Hell?" I look around for some mode of transport, but I can't see any cars or trains, nor is there a stable for horses.

Kerry grimaces. "It differs depending on what frame of mind Lucifer and Hell itself are in."

All the guys except for Teddy start muttering about how crazy Lucifer's whims can be, but I ignore them and choose to pay attention to my friend. She is the one most up to date on everything Hell, but it's not Kerry who answers.

"This way, my lady, if you don't mind." Cerberus leaps up and prances toward the nearby building, his middle head doing the talking.

We all follow behind the crazy animal, Teddy making sure the girls are far away from him. They seem to have the same crazy mood swings a sloth demon is prone to. God knows my brothers were a handful growing up, and don't get me started on the hormonal messes they were during puberty. Thankfully I had moved away from home by then, but going to visit was like walking in a minefield.

The entrance slides back at Cerberus's approach, and I come to a full stop the moment I see what's inside.

"Segways are the current mode of transportation here," Cerberus announces with a flourish of a front paw.

Lined up before us are rows upon rows of those infernal contraptions that I swore I was never going to ever ride on, and I wonder how we are going to survive this part of the trip.

Chapter Nine

"**F**uck." I'm so shocked, I forget about the little ears listening.

"That's a dollar for the swear jar, Mom," Aria says, still a little teary. The right head gasps, and Cerberus drops to his belly again, and then wiggle crawls toward the little girls.

"We are sorry we scared the little munchkins. We love children and would never eat them, only bad adults," the right head says, fluttering its eyelashes at the little girls.

"Please forgive us," the middle head pleads, and the left head huffs but looks at the two girls hopefully.

They look at their dad for support, and he seems unsure.

"We would never hurt Nolan's children. Julian says it's not their fault their father is an asshat," the left head says helpfully.

Nolan glares at them but nods his approval to the girls, who crouch down and giggle as Cerberus rolls over, exposing their pink belly to the girls. They both give it a scratch, and they wriggle like a worm, doing that same purr cough they did when I gave them scratches behind the ears.

"I can't ride one of those." Teddy shakes his head, pointing at the confounded machines. "My balance is terrible."

"Neither can the girls," I point out. They are all sized for adults, so neither of the girls can see over the handlebars.

"Relax, Lucifer had to make some adjustments when he realized how difficult a fuc—damn Segway was to ride. You can't see them, but in the back rows, there are a couple of electric cars. Only people with children are allowed to use them."

"Why don't you drive that, Teddy, and take the girls with you?" Nolan suggests, heaving a sigh of relief.

"But he's just twisted enough to make everyone else ride them. He likes to sit on the balcony of the palace and watch disaster happen as everyone tries to go to work in the morning," Kerry says. "Sometimes, he even puts an obstacle course up overnight just to make it even more interesting."

"Lucifer is an asshole," I mutter quietly so I don't owe the swear jar more money.

"You have no idea," Kerry mutters back to me.

"Thank you. If it had been a motorcycle, it would have been no problem, but I just don't have the right coordination for that."

"Motorcycles were the mode of transport last

time I was here," Louis says, shuddering. "Thankfully, Felix was with me, and I rode bitch while he drove." Felix is Louis's brother, and he's married to Nolan's sister Bella.

"Not a fan, I take it?" Teddy chuckles, and Louis shakes his head.

"No, I like to be enclosed when moving at high speeds."

"I remember a long period of horseback riding when I was a kid," Carter says as he straps a helmet to his head. "Thankfully, he allowed a horse and carriage to be used around the city so we didn't actually have to ride."

"Ugh, yes, and you had to be careful where you walked in the street in case one of the horses pooped. That shit would literally burn through your shoes." Mason groans, reminiscing. "He had to employ people specifically to go around and clean up, and they got hazard pay because the poop was so dangerous. There were a few demons who got rich during that period of travel."

"Okay, shall we get going then?" I ask, heading over to one of the Segways, ignoring the crazy reminiscing. I'm sure I'll have some of my own stories to tell about my seemingly mad uncle soon enough. "We may as well try it. Let's hope we make it to the city in one piece and injury free."

"Safety first." Cerberus jumps to their feet and bounds over to the wall where helmets hang. One of his heads lifts one, and they bound back, sliding to a halt in front of me, wagging their tail. They place the helmet in my hands. The middle head swipes a tongue across the plain black helmet, and it changes to rainbow glitter. The girls jump up and down with excitement when they see it.

"Mom, your helmet is so pretty!" Zoe shouts, pointing at it.

"Whoa, how did you do that?" I ask, and their whole-body shrugs.

"Magic," they say, and all three heads wink at me.

"Stop flirting with Glory," Kerry scolds, and they stick their tongues out at her.

"Can we just get moving please?" Nolan sounds exasperated and not just a little bit annoyed.

Everyone else finds themselves a helmet and a Segway, and Nolan straps the girls into the back of Teddy's electric car. There are no car seats, but Kerry assures him there will be no other traffic on the road—well, not cars anyway. It's decided that Nolan will ride with them as well. We are going to stop by his parents' place on the way to the palace. Apparently, it's on the outskirts of the city, and it would be silly to go in and come back out again.

They set off, telling us they'll wait until we get there. I sigh wistfully as the car disappears down the only road, not looking forward to my own journey at all.

"Can't we just take the other electric cars?" Ben whines, and I have to say, I'm in full support.

"Sure, if you want to be noticed and dragged kicking and screaming directly to the palace. I, for one, am happier with the plan to avoid Lucifer for as long as possible." Kerry steps up onto her Segway and easily balances on the spot. "Now, remember Segways have no brakes, it's all in the back and forth lean of your body."

"No brakes?" Mason sounds horrified, and from the look on the others' faces, they are too.

"Relax, you're demons. We take to this shit like ducks to water, you'll see." Kerry's biting her lip as she says this, and I'm almost certain she's trying not to laugh.

"Let's go." Cerberus bounds off down the road, and the rest of us follow at a much slower pace. It takes us all a mile or so to work out the mechanics of these stupid machines, but soon enough, we are mostly stable. Cerberus doesn't seem to get winded, and he appears to be enjoying the exercise, his tongue hanging out. I kind of wish we had full helmets instead of these bicycle ones, because more than once, an insect flew into my mouth while I was chatting, and we had to stop so I could cough it up. I wasn't the only one.

"Now that I'm comfortable, let's talk about why you are so keen to avoid Lucifer?" I say to my friend, who doesn't take her eyes off the road.

"Oh, I thought that was what you wanted." She doesn't look at me, and I can tell she's hiding something.

"I mean, I kind of do, but there seems to be more to it than just that. Is there something I need to know? Please don't let me walk into a meeting with my uncle without all the facts."

She sighs and eases back on the speed a little. The guys pull farther ahead, and I know they can't hear us when she says, "Lucifer claims I'm his mate, and I have been avoiding letting him touch me for about, oh, two years." She says these words so fast that it takes me a moment to decipher them.

"Oh!" I finally work out what she says. "That's big."

"Yeah, it is, but I really don't want to be trapped in Hell, which is what will happen if I mate with Lucifer. What the majority of the population doesn't know is that his two lieutenants are also his mates. Before they were mated, they were able to leave Hell and keep an eye on Earth bound demons for Luc, but since their bonds snapped into place, they are also tied to the land."

"And you don't want to be tied to the land and trapped in Hell?"

She shakes her head. "No, I love traveling to Earth, and now that I have Nolan and Carter's course under my belt, I can do it in a work capacity as well."

"So you don't like him? What's wrong? Is he ugly?"

Kerry scoffs. "Please, not a single person in your family could ever be called unattractive, let alone ugly. He's fucking hot and sexy, but he's also used to getting his own way and people bowing down before him. I don't know if I can be that person."

"I'm sure he needs someone to tell him no. He may even relish it."

"I think he does. We've been playing a game of cat and mouse for two years. It's one of the reasons I wanted Cerberus to keep his mouth shut. Thankfully, he's distracted keeping an eye on Ben at the moment and won't return to the palace until you do."

"Ah, so you're throwing Ben to the wolves, so to speak."

"For now. I'm sorry, Glory. I know he's your mate, but I'm not ready to trust him either. For all we know, he could be completely loyal to Mabuz, and this is a scheme to get him where he needs to be, so this works out for all of us."

I sigh, my gaze moving to Ben. He's next to Louis, and he keeps offering suggestions every time he wobbles back and forth. It's kind of cute actually, but Kerry is right. He could be the snake in the grass.

The ride to the outskirts of the city takes about half an hour. The Segways really move quickly in a straight line, and that's exactly what the road is. There are a few gentle curves, but it's mostly straight and flat without side roads. The land is much the same through the whole journey—wide open, grassy plains with livestock grazing just like you would find on Earth. Occasionally, we see a farm dwelling, but there is no other traffic on the road except for us.

Once we hit the city limits, the amount of traffic picks up a little. People smile and nod as they pass by on their own Segways, these ones more personalized to the owner with various colors and paint jobs, but I guess it isn't really easy to personalize something so basic. Side roads appear to lead into housing developments. I try to peer down one to get a better look, but that sends my Segway careening sideways, almost taking out Kerry as well, so I decide forward facing is the safest place to be.

Carter takes a turn left into one of the side streets, and we follow behind. This street seems to be made up of large blocks, with big backyards and lush gardens. There are large trees and even larger houses. Every now and then, I catch sight of swimming pools in the backyards. Carter turns into a cobblestone driveway, and my teeth chatter violently as our Segways bounce across the uneven surface. Finally, we stop next to the little electric car that Teddy drove Nolan and the girls in.

"Fucking hell, Lucifer is a menace. That was fucking awful," Mason complains as he pulls his Segway to a stop and jumps down.

The rest of us do the same, and I'd like to say it was all well-coordinated and smooth, but that would be a lie. Louis literally drives his onto the grass and throws himself off it, tucking and rolling as he hits the ground.

He groans and gets to his feet. "That's it, I'll walk the rest of the way if I have to. I am not getting back on that thing."

He really struggled the most, and I don't blame him for being annoyed. I manage to get mine to stop, but the lack of brakes makes me wary about getting off. I look around for some help. Carter, Kerry, and Ben are all on their feet, having had no problems getting on or off. I think I secretly hate all three of them, but before I can ask for help, Ben approaches me.

"Can I give you a hand?" He grabs hold of the handlebars. I feel a rush of affection, which I know is the mate bond pushing for us to seal it, but we need a conversation before that happens, and now is not the time.

"Thank you, I wasn't sure if I was going to have to copy Louis or not." While he steadies it, I step off it. "And I'm pretty sure I couldn't tuck and roll quite so elegantly."

"Glory, I think we need to talk," he says quietly just as the front door to the house opens and Zoe and Aria come running out.

I sigh. God, I feel like I've spent all day sighing. "Yes, we probably do, but it's going to have to wait for a little while longer. Let's get the girls settled, and I'll make some time for you a little later."

He bites his lip and looks like he's going to argue but nods and returns to his Segway. My eyes narrow as I watch him rub his chest exactly where his mark from Mabuz is. Is that a subconscious thing, or is he being summoned and it's hurting? I'm about to ask when Nolan calls me over.

"Glory, come and meet my mom and dad."

Turning, I find an older version of Nolan and his sister Bella. They are busy greeting Carter and Louis and being introduced to Mason and Ben, but they finally turn their attention to me.

I was expecting a bit of hesitation, being that we've never met before, but I'm swept up into the hugs and greetings like a long-lost daughter.

"Glory, it's so wonderful to finally meet you. Nolan and the girls have told us so much about you." Evelyn kisses my cheeks before pulling back to look at me at arm's length. "You have no idea what a relief it is that our boys have found their mate, and the girls have a kind and loving mother. We have been so worried about them, but being confined to Hell and only allowed to visit twice a year has made it so much worse."

"I would have paid a small fortune to see you smack that she-beast in the face with a shovel." Gregor, Nolan's dad, nudges his wife out of the way and gives me a big hug before beaming at me. His eyes flash with the telltale red of a wrath demon. "I bet it was glorious, if you'll pardon the pun."

I look around to make sure the girls are occupied. They are busy throwing a ball for Cerberus, who seems thrilled to chase after it and bring it back to them. "I can assure you it certainly was," I admit without any shame. "If I could find her now, I'd happily use Sparky on her too."

"Sparky?" Gregor asks, looking confused.

"Her taser, Dad. She's a menace with it," Nolan explains, putting an arm around my shoulders and hugging me into his side.

"Yeah, she got Nolan and me with it. We went down like sacks of shit." Carter takes my other side and gives me a little pinch on the ass.

I glare at them. "Well that will teach you to mess with me."

"Good for you, Glory, teaching them that you are the boss of the household. I like it." Evelyn chuckles. "Now, are you all going to come inside for some drinks and nibbles?"

"Unfortunately we can't. We don't want to draw any attention here if we can avoid it and I don't think our arrival was as unobtrusive as I had hoped." Nolan nods in the direction of the neighbors, who have come outside to be nosy and are staring in shock at Lucifer's gatekeeper playing fetch with the girls.

"Crap, that's not good," I mutter. I wonder how long it's going to take until news of our arrival makes the rounds of Hell. We may be on my uncle's radar much sooner than I hoped for.

Chapter Ten

"Pfft, that's just Karen and Terry. Nobody likes them, so they wouldn't have anyone to tell anyway." Gregor raises his hand for what I think is going to be a wave, but he flips them off instead. "Fuck you, Terry. May your cock turn green and fall off."

My mouth drops open in surprise.

Behind me somewhere, I hear Mason laugh out loud. "I think I'm going to like being in this family."

"Christ, are you still feuding?" Nolan shakes his head in exasperation as both Karen and Terry give their own rude gestures back before going inside and slamming their door.

"Yes, they won't take care of the fire snails in their garden, and they come onto our property and set fire to all my prized Earth roses. Do you know how long I had to baby them to get used to Hell's soil?" Nolan's father complains, and I giggle at his petulant pout.

Evelyn just rolls her eyes. "Now don't you worry about a thing. Nolan and Theo explained every-thing, dear. We will keep the girls here for as long as necessary. You make sure you take care of yourself and your boys. I can't say how thrilling it is to have one of the first septimax in hundreds of years in the family."

"Septimax?" I repeat, not entirely sure what she's talking about. "That sounds like a freaking transformer."

"Yes, and you are a septimax prime with a full complement of sins as mates. It used to happen more frequently, but it happened less and less until it never happened. I think it's been two hundred years since the last one passed on."

"Passed on?"

"Yes, a septimax will all die at the same time, so once you are bonded to all your mates, if one of you were to fall sick, you all would. If one of you got hit by a train, then the rest would die instantly. One can't exist without the others. I think it's kind of romantic." She sighs happily like it's the most romantic thing she's ever heard, but I'm just plain horrified. I've tied all these men to me, and now we are mortally linked. I've doomed them if Bridgette and Mabuz get their way, but wait, there are only six of us so far.

"And this is a lust demon trait?" I ask her, and she shakes her head, smiling with twinkling eyes.

"No, Glory, it was strictly Gluttony demons who would have all seven sins as mates."

Ah, okay, now that actually makes a lot more

sense. I'm like a Pokémon trainer, and I have to catch them all.

"But I don't have a sloth mate, so I don't think we count as a septimax." I can hear the desperation in my voice, but either she doesn't hear it or ignores it, unaware of my inner turmoil.

"Never say never. Have you come across a sloth demon recently?"

I think about it, but the only sloth demons I've knowingly interacted with are my brothers. "Not that I know of," I admit with relief, but she beams.

"See? It may still happen. Maybe we should arrange a dinner with some of the more eligible sloth demons we know. Oh, that would be a wonderful idea. What do you think?" She gets enthusiastic, but I start to panic, and Louis picks up on it. He must see it on my face.

"Evie, how about we hold off on that for the time being. We wouldn't want to drag anyone else into the danger we're in," he says diplomatically, and if I don't have a seventh mate, surely all the others will be just fine if something happens to me.

She frowns but nods. "True, but I'm still going to write a list so that once you have taken care of everything, we can have a little party before you return to Earth." Cerberus catches her eye. "It's such a shame that Julian became the host for the gate keeper. He would have been a perfect sloth mate for you. He and Nolan were best friends for so long, their falling out was devastating for us all, but now he's tied to Hell anyway. He wouldn't be able to leave to go back to Earth with you."

My eyes drift to the dog, who has sprawled out on the grass under a tree, all three tongues hanging out of his muzzles. They are letting the girls poke flowers into the spaces between their ridges. Cerberus looks like something out of a Disney movie, all covered in pretty flowers. I had forgotten that he is a sloth demon. Kerry said he shifts, but I haven't seen evidence of this being true. He seems perfectly happy in dog form. Maybe it's for the best. He seems to be holding quite a grudge against Nolan, so I doubt he would be all that thrilled to meet me, despite Kerry thinking that Cerberus was flirting with me.

We quickly give the girls hugs and kisses good-bye. Not a single one of us is left out of the hug fest. Ben looks gobsmacked when both girls hug his legs and tell him they'll miss him.

"I am not getting back on that contraption," Louis says once the others go inside, crossing his arms stubbornly and nodding at the Segway still lying on the grass.

Nolan chuckles at our partner and puts his arm around him, giving him a sideways hug. Louis winces. Maybe he didn't come off the Segway as gracefully as I thought. "Shit, are you hurt?" Nolan loses his amusement and spins to face Louis, but he shakes his head.

"No, only a few bumps and bruises and mostly my pride," he admits. Nolan leans in and gives him a kiss on the lips, and Cerberus starts to growl again.

"Oh, stop. If Julian has something to say, he can come out and say it to my face, but I'm guessing he's too gutless because then he would have to admit he was just as much to blame for whatever happened between us as I am." Nolan's eyes flash red, and the two of them have a stare down before Cerberus huffs and turns his back on us.

"How about you ride with Teddy, babe, and I'll take the Segway? Now that the girls are gone, I don't mind riding along with the others.

"Would you?" Louis's eyes light up with relief, and he starts talking rapidly in French, hugging and kissing Nolan in between. You would think having a French speaking mother, I would have picked up the language, but I just had no ear for it. Serena did, and she speaks French beautifully. I can understand a few words here and there, but I butcher it if I try to speak it.

We are finally on our way again. Ben elects to go in the car as well so as not to draw attention to himself. Apparently, there are palace guards patrolling the street, and they sometimes stop you and ask for ID. Kerry thinks if they see us with Cerberus, we'll definitely be stopped. She says she's taking us the most indirect route to their home, so that we don't have to pass by the front of the palace.

Cerberus looks torn between jumping into the back of the little car and running along with us, but in the end, he stays with us. I'm almost certain his large body wouldn't fit in there anyway despite Ben's slender form.

The trip through the city is cumbersome. There is a lot more traffic, and it's harder to manipulate the Segways when other people are zooming around you. We are considerably slower than all the natives who have been riding them for years. I guess we are a little conspicuous with our inexperienced handling, and we get a few strange looks and a lot of glares. The fact that there is a giant, three-headed dog bounding along with us probably doesn't help. Kerry keeps hissing at him to stick to the shadows, but he seems happy to ignore her and do his own thing.

As we travel through the city, I desperately want to look around and take it all in. It looks like a mash-up of old and new, much like London, but I'm also not particularly confident that I can do that and stay on track. We pass under a number of electronic billboards just floating in the sky, and my curiosity wins out over safety.

"What are those?" I ask, not wanting to take my

hands off the handles to gesture to them, so I use my head, but of course that throws me off balance. I go careening to the side, narrowly missing a cart selling produce on the side of the street. The seller shakes his hand and curses at me as his customers jump out of my way.

"Fuck," I scream as I yank my yoke up so hard I start spinning in circles. Round and round I go without a clue how to stop myself.

"Cut it out, Glory, you're drawing attention," Kerry snaps at me as a small crowd gathers to stare at my pirouette.

"I would if I could," I shout at her before groaning. My head is spinning, and I'm starting to feel a little nauseous.

Suddenly, my Segway stops as a hand snaps out and grabs hold of it, but I don't. My body, now dizzy as shit, just tumbles off the side. I can see the sidewalk rapidly approaching, but I'm suddenly scooped up and cradled against a hard chest. I look up into the brightest lavender eyes I have ever seen, almost the color of violets, and they are breathtaking. The man who came to my rescue has white blond hair that falls around his shoulders, sharp cheekbones, and a slightly pointed nose. He's so pretty, he looks like an elf from *Lord of the Rings*.

"Thank you." I blink a few times to make sure that the dizziness has gone, and I'm not seeing things, but sure enough, the pretty man stays where he is. A lock of his silvery blond hair falls over his face, so I reach up and push it back, brushing my hand across his cheek. A pinch of pain in my hand signals I've found my final mate—sloth. Of course I have.

"For fuck's sake, Julian. If it wasn't bad enough that fucking dog was bounding around with us, now you have to go and shift in public. We were trying to go incognito," Kerry bitches from somewhere behind me.

My eyes widen in shock. This is Kerry's brother? They look nothing alike. She's dark and Latina looking, and he is most definitely not.

He ignores his sister's grouching and looks as shocked as I am. "Mate?" He sounds confused. Suddenly, we're surrounded by my other three nearby mates.

"What the fuck?" Nolan demands, sounding annoyed, but the shock in Julian's face turns to smugness, and he helps me stand upright.

"I fucking told you we were mates." He looks at his hand before holding it out for us all to see. Sure enough, he has seven colored rings around his sloth designation, and I am officially a septimax prime, whatever that entails. Hopefully it's just a fancy word for a demon with seven mates and not anything else, but I'm just annoyed.

"Great, so that confirms that at least four out of my seven mates were man-whores prior to me.

Maybe I should have had you all tested for STIs before I let any of you stick your dicks in me."

Julian still has one arm wrapped around me, but it's Mason who answers.

"Demons don't have STIs, and I have been with Teddy for two years, and previous to that, I was with Mathias for six."

"Well, don't you get a gold sticker?" Carter grumbles.

"Why is he naked?" Mason asks, sounding amused, and it's only then that I realize the man holding me is indeed stark naked, and my body is nestled against his. We are so close, in fact, that I can't even get a good look at my new mate's goodies.

"Because he's an idiot, and he forgets he can't shift with clothes on, so he's always naked when he shifts back into human form. It's most definitely a downside," Kerry says, pushing into the group surrounding us and holding out a set of clothes. "I've started keeping a spare set in my interdimensional cubby because he thinks that people enjoy seeing him naked, but I assure you, I don't."

It's almost like Julian is reluctant to let me go, but he does and takes the shirt and sweats his sister gives him before yawning and pushing his long hair back off his face.

He quickly pulls his clothes on before turning his gaze on Nolan. "You're looking well," he says, but he sounds disappointed. His bland stare turns to a sneer as he looks at Carter. "You're such a hypocrite. You called me a man-whore and then hooked up with this one." He nods at Carter who blanches but doesn't deny it.

"The difference between you and them is that we all had an understanding. We were open and honest with the fact that we were seeing other people. Carter needed it for his sin, and both Louis and I enjoy the company of women as well as each other. They never hid anything from me, and I them. You did, or tried to anyway, and you would chase off anyone who showed the slightest interest in me. Essentially, you were cockblocking and gate-keeping and not doing the same for yourself. You would say we were mates and you wanted me to yourself but didn't have enough respect for me to grant me the same. You wanted to have your cake and eat it too. "

"Okay, it's obvious that the two of you have some air to clear, but can we not do it here?" Kerry sounds almost panicked. She glances to the left of us, where there is a large landscaped park with lots of trees, but on the other side of the park I can see a palace-like building.

"Is that the palace?" I ask, and she nods.

"Yes, and sometimes, Luc likes to walk in the backyard, so can we please get moving?"

"How far do we have to go? I don't think I can

get back on that thing." I point to the Segway standing innocently where Julian left it when he caught me.

"Not far, just walk, but hurry," she urges, gets back on her Segway, and takes off up the street, parallel to the park.

"Are you okay walking with him?" Mason eyes Julian with curiosity, but so far, he has kept his mouth closed.

"Yes, I'm fine." I wave him off, and he and Carter get back on their machines. Carter has stayed suspiciously quiet, which worries me.

"Will you look after her?" Nolan asks Julian, who rolls his eyes and sighs dramatically.

"Like she was my own mate. Oh, wait, she is. Now fuck off, Nolan. I'm not ready to forgive you."

Nolan splutters incoherently, and his eyes flash red with wrath before he spins on the spot and stomps back to his machine.

"You've really pissed him off now," I mutter out of the side of my mouth.

"You're welcome," he says just as quietly as he gallantly holds out his arm for me.

I slip my hand around his arm but frown at him. "What do you mean, you're welcome?"

"Well, angry sex with Nolan is sublime, don't you think?" He winks a lavender eye and pulls me along while I just gape at him in shock.

"Did you do all that he accused you of, just so

he would angry fuck you?" I ask, and he shrugs, and the smirk turns sheepish.

"Look, I never claimed to be smart. I just didn't want him to leave me, and I ended up pushing him away anyway. All of those people he accuses me of fucking were mostly rumors. I paid someone to start them, and you know what college gossip is like, it snowballed. Before I knew it, I had a bigger reputation than I planned. I just didn't think he would get so angry that he would leave. I was hoping I could trigger the mate mark to form. I always had this feeling, but I guess we were missing our prime and that was why it never happened."

"Why are you pissed then? You are a product of your own making."

"Because he was my best friend. He was never supposed to leave. He was never supposed to find that one and the chef." He nods in Carter's direction. "Let alone have children with that woman." He sounds defeated, and while it's his own fault, I can't help feeling sorry for him.

"Well, that was out of his control, and you saw firsthand how adorable they are," I remind him, and his lips turn up in a small grin.

"Cerberus liked them, and they were cute. The little one was sad he didn't have fur she could brush, but both of them smelled scared. Why is that?"

"God, Julian, there is so much to catch you up

on, but let's get inside and stop your sister from freaking out. I can see her glaring at us."

"That's only because she knows she's run out of luck. Luc said next time she came back, there would be no escaping. Shit is about to get real. There will be no escaping for her. He spent hundreds of years being lonely and finding his other two mates helped, he felt incomplete. While he has enjoyed playing cat and mouse with her, he's done."

Chapter Eleven

"**H**undreds of years? How is he so old? I know demons live three times the length of humans, but that seems to be extreme," I ask my new mate as we approach a lavish town house.

The others have already gone inside. Kerry hustled them off the street in a flurry of panic. I can see the little electric car is also parked in front of the house. It's not the only car, but it is the only one without a protective cover over it. I guess people didn't want their cars to go to waste in case Lucifer ever decided to bring back that mode of transportation.

"Luc's life force is tied to the land. As long as he is the ruler of Hell, he will keep living," he explains, pushing open the door and stepping back, allowing me to walk in.

"And when he stops being the ruler, he'll just shrivel up and die? That's horrible."

Julian chuckles at my outrage. "No, his life force will run a normal course from the day the new heir is crowned, giving him many happy years with his mates."

"Is my mother that old? And speaking of that, do they have parents? Or did he just appear out of thin air? How did Lucifer become the ruler of Hell?" I pepper him with questions.

"Whoa, slow down. I'm good friends with your uncle, especially since I became Cerberus's host. He considers me family for saving his companion, but even I don't know the answers to some of those questions. He's very tight-lipped about his origins, but I'm sure he will tell you everything."

I've been too distracted to look around the house, but we arrive in a large, cozy living area. All around the room are photos of Kerry and Julian and two people who must be their mom and dad. I can see why they look so different now. Julian is the spitting image of his mother, and Kerry takes after her father, though she is a pretty feminine version.

There is a low-key conversation going on between Nolan, Carter, and Louis. Kerry and Ben are nowhere to be seen, and Teddy and Mason have turned the TV on and are trying to discreetly ignore the other three, but Mason is a snoop, and I can see he has his eyes on the TV and his ears on the conversation. It makes me smile.

There's a brief silence as they notice our entry and stop talking.

"Well, this is awkward. I'm starving, what's there to eat?" I ask, ignoring all the other problems we have accumulated.

"I'm not much of a cook," Julian warns.

"I'll say," Nolan mutters sarcastically, but apart from flipping him off, Julian ignores him.

"But I have a large collection of takeout menus. What do you feel like? I'll place an order."

"Something spicy," I tell him. "There's nothing I won't try at least once."

He smirks. "That's good to know."

"Stop flirting with my mate," Nolan snaps, and my eyebrows rise in surprise.

"She's my mate too, asshole." A sly gleam glitters in Julian's eyes. "In fact, they all are. I could kiss any of them if I wanted, and guess what? You couldn't say a word."

To my and everyone else's surprise, Nolan bursts into flames.

"Holy shit," Carter stares with wide-eyed amazement.

"Whoa, hey, how about we all take five? Maybe rustle up some drinks and talk about this rationally?" Teddy jumps to his feet and steps between Nolan and Julian.

Louis braves the fire, but it doesn't burn him, and with a few carefully placed strokes and whispered words, the flames die out.

"Fuck, I'm surrounded by children, and the two actual children in this family aren't even here. I don't need this shit. There is too much going on. I'm going to leave the five of you here and maybe you can civilly fill Julian in on everything while I go speak to my other problematic mate," I announce just as Kerry returns.

"Ben is settled into a room upstairs. He looked like he was about to bolt at any second, so I suggested he take a nap or a shower or something." She looks just as frazzled as she makes Ben sound.

"Why don't you take your own advice? These idiots don't need you to babysit them." I wave a frustrated hand at said idiots, and she glares at them.

"Don't burn my fucking parents' house down or destroy anything, otherwise, you're paying for it. And Julian, just try not to be... you."

Her brother rolls his eyes but makes himself comfortable on a single recliner, putting the foot rest up before reaching into his interdimensional cubby and pulling out some takeaway menus. That's followed by a cell phone.

"Relax, dear sister. I'm just going to order some food and drinks, and everything will be fine, I promise." He yawns. "Then I might have a little nap. You know how shifting makes me tired."

She scoffs. "You're a sloth demon, breathing makes you tired," she retorts at the same time as Nolan sneers, "Is there anything that doesn't make you tired?"

I roll my eyes. This is a mess.

Julian pretends to think about it and shrugs.

"No, not really, but maybe your lust demon would like to come over and join me on my chair, and maybe we can recharge both of us. I always sleep so much better after I come."

Nolan growls before bursting into flames again and lunges toward Julian. Teddy, Carter, and Louis shout and try to intercept him while Mason just rolls his eyes and gets up.

"As much as I enjoy the drama, maybe now isn't the right time for it. Sort your shit out before our mate goes to her uncle and asks him to dissolve all the bonds."

"Really fucking tempted right now," I admit sadly.

It seems like my new mate might not be able to get over his grudge despite it being his own fault, and Nolan is completely irrational. Poor Louis and Carter don't really know how to react. I wonder if they knew about Julian. Surely it's something they would have talked about in the past. Neither of them looked particularly surprised to hear it, but Nolan's wrath is out of control, and I think that's surprising them. He is usually so balanced.

Mason turns his back on them and follows Kerry and me out of the room. "Come on, let's go find our other wayward mate and see where he's at and if his meltdown is any less dramatic than this one."

"You're being awfully calm about all of this," I

comment as Kerry leads us up a set of stairs. "You seem to have gotten over your distrust of Ben."

He shakes his head. "Not in the least, which is why I wanted to accompany you. I don't trust him not to manipulate you. You're so kind and loving, and you want to see the good in everyone," he confesses, and I guess it won't hurt. He's right, I do try to see the best in everyone.

"Ben's in there. He really was beside himself when he got here, muttering about being summoned. I think it won't be long before Mabuz knows he's missing," Kerry tells us, pointing at a nearby door. "As much as I want to avoid Luc, I don't think you should for much longer. He's the only one I know who is going to be able to help you with your Mabuz problem. He's the only demon strong enough to possibly defeat the blood magic Mabuz is wielding."

I pull her in for a quick hug, and she looks startled for a moment but sags into me with a sigh. "Maybe we can hide the fact you're here," I suggest, but she shakes her head.

"Do you remember when I was arguing with Cerberus and one of his sets of eyes turned green?" she asks, and I nod. It was just before I thought he was going to rip her face off.

"That was Luc seeing through his eyes. He already knows I'm here, but he's making me sweat, the predator after the prey. He thinks it's a fun game. If I try to make it back to the portal now, I will be intercepted."

"Crap, well, when I go to visit him, I will distract him as long as possible. You can take the electric car and at least try to get back to Earth. I know you don't want to be trapped here. Maybe one day a Hell heir will appear, and he will be able to come to you."

"I'm not holding my breath for either thing, but thank you for trying to make me feel better. You have more important things to worry about, though, than making me feel better. You have your own mate shit sandwich."

"Thanks for reminding me," I deadpan, trying to obliterate her with my eyes, but she remains in one piece.

"Well, at least I'm not suffering alone." Kerry gives me a little finger wave and wanders farther down the hallway, disappearing into another bedroom.

"Come on, let's go see what kind of meltdown Ben is having." Mason knocks on the door and steps back, pushing me in front. "You go first, I don't want to intimidate him."

"Honestly, I got the impression that you didn't," I retort, and he grins.

"I know, I do love brats. Hopefully when he gets over his anxiety and worry about the benefactor, his bratty self will come out to play."

"Oh, remind me to show you the playroom at home. I'm sure you'll find that as fun as the club. I kind of want to avoid it now that my brother is the dungeon master." He chuckles as I shudder, and then he leans in and gives me a kiss on the cheek as a muffled voice yells, "Come in."

"Can't wait," he promises, and we enter the room. It's just a bedroom, and it's empty, but I can hear muttering coming from the attached bathroom. We exchange a glance.

"Ben, is everything okay?" I call out.

"No, everything is not," he replies and suddenly appears in the bathroom doorway.

My eyes widen in surprise, because he's mostly naked except for a pair of tight boxer briefs. Mason makes an appreciative noise next to me, and I don't blame him. He has sleek muscles that are covered by a layer of pretty pale skin, flawless apart from the red brand on his chest. Ben has a full face of makeup on, his smoky eye artfully applied, and he's wearing his gorgeous red Poppy wig, but he holds his hand out, and it's shaking.

"My hand is shaking so badly, I can't apply my eyelashes. My favorite boobs and hip padding are at the club, and my dick takes one look at you two and refuses to be tucked. I'm a freaking mess. Mabuz could track me down at any second, and if I'm not in my Poppy persona, I'll be punished."

He bursts into tears, and I hurry over to him,

guiding him to the bed where I put my arms around him and hold him tight.

"Oh, sweetie, it's okay. We're going to get this all taken care of," I assure him, rubbing my hands over his back, his skin silky smooth beneath my palms.

Mason sits on the bed, frowning. "Why do you think he'll find you soon?" he asks gently, and I brush his hair back as he lifts his tearstained face off my shoulder.

"The brand is summoning me. I must have gone off his radar. It only burns a little, but I know within a few hours, it will be unbearable. I will have no choice but to return to Earth if I want the pain to stop." He hiccups as Mason and I exchange a glance.

"I think I probably know how to stop it, but first, I need to ask a question." Mason sounds so serious, it even stops Ben's tears. "Were you telling us the complete truth about everything?"

Ben nods emphatically, his red hair swinging. "Absolutely. I hate him." His voice drops, as do his eyes, and he won't look at us. "I hate some of the things he makes me do. I'm not a pet, I don't like to sit by his feet and beg for attention." When his eyes lift, they are blazing with anger. "I deserve to be treated better."

"Of course you do," I coo to him. "No one should be made to feel like shit."

"And there is nothing else you're hiding?"

Mason presses, and when Ben bites his lip, I know he's about to tell us something disturbing.

"Mabuz is the reason Cerberus became sick. He couldn't get to Lucifer, so he attacked the closest thing. He was livid when Lucifer found a way around it by having someone host Cerberus's soul. He thought it would weaken Luc enough to be able to wrestle Hell from him."

I breathe a small sigh of relief. At least it was nothing about Ben, just more Mabuz intel, which is a good thing.

"I was too scared to tell you that around Cerberus earlier."

Mason chuckles. "I understand, kid, but I think you'll change your mind once you see what he looks like now." Mason winks, and Ben frowns in confusion. "Don't worry, we'll introduce you later. Now, I think the most important question is, do you really want to be Glory's mate? I think sealing the bond would be a way to override that." Mason nods at the ugly red brand on his chest. Again, Ben bites nervously at his lip, and I brace myself for whatever is going to come out of his mouth.

Chapter Twelve

"I just don't understand how I am Glory's mate. I haven't had a girlfriend in years." Ben sounds confused and frustrated.

"So you're gay?" Mason asks, his brow wrinkling, and I'm not sure it's in disappointment on my behalf or confusion, maybe a combination of both. I know that's what I'm feeling, and add in hurt because nobody likes to hear that their mate doesn't want them. Surely fate wouldn't give me a gay mate. That would be cruel to both of us.

"Well, yeah, I guess." He doesn't sound so sure, and I really don't have the patience for this at the moment.

"Look, you're either into pussy or you're not. Have you had sex with a woman before?" Mason is still taking the lead on this, and I am extremely thankful for it.

Ben's eyes drop, and he shrugs. "I've made out with a few, but I think I was more interested in their clothes, shoes, and makeup. I gave up on women when they were jealous because I looked better in their clothes than they did."

"So you've had sex with men?" I ask, and he nods.

"Yeah, of course."

"Did you enjoy making out with those women? Did your dick get hard?" Mason asks, and I almost can't believe we're having this conversation.

"Yeah, but I was a teenage boy, so my dick got hard with a stiff breeze." Ben shrugs, and I giggle at the description… then I have an idea.

"So is it my pussy that's the problem? Because I have another hole you can use, you know? If you want to be the one being penetrated, I don't mind doing some experimenting. I always wanted to give pegging a try but haven't been game enough to ask any of the guys yet." I pull out my phone and start googling pegging and strap-on harness. I wonder if you can use vegetables in a strap on harness. I remember seeing some nice cobs of corn at the supermarket, and I bet they'd feel good.

I realize the room is silent and the conversation hasn't continued. When I look up, both Ben and Mason are staring at me with disbelief, but then Mason erupts into laughter, laughing so hard he rolls off the bed and onto the floor with a thump.

"Well, that was an… interesting offer, Glory." Ben seems unsure of what he wants to say.

"Well, I mean it's not our fault that this happened, and I'm willing to try other options if you are." I'm trying to make the best of a bad situation. "But if you really want out, we can ask Luc to dissolve the mating when we go see him." I feel a little sad about this option, but I soldier on. "But I just want you to know that I'm not sad or upset at having Ben or even Poppy Cox as my mate. I would take you whichever way you are more comfortable, and I'm pretty sure no one else here cares either way."

Mason is still rolling on the floor with laughter, so he can't comment, but it doesn't matter, because Ben is looking at me with eyes shiny with tears once more.

"But you have to be in the right place for you, and if this isn't it, then it's never going to work."

Ben narrows his eyes in contemplation. "It doesn't bother you that I dress up as Poppy Cox and may be more interested in your mates than you?"

I shrug my shoulders. "I won't lie and say I'm not disappointed, because I am, but if you're worried because you think I'm going to judge you for liking men, well, the five that I am mated to fuck men as often as they fuck me. As long as I'm included or at least asked to join in, I don't really care either way. Who am I to judge you for your sexual orientation? I just want you to be happy."

The light shining in his eyes is nothing short of grateful, and before I can say anything else to assure him that I like him just the way he is, he leans forward and kisses me. I'm so shocked it takes me a moment to react, and he almost pulls away, but I wrap my arms around him and pull him down onto the bed on top of me, returning his kiss enthusiastically. I can't stop my hands from wandering all over the smooth, silky skin of his back. He feels so different from the other guys, like he moisturizes everything daily. When he pulls away, he's breathless and panting hard.

"Anything?" I ask him, and he groans.

"God, yes." He kisses me again and grinds against me.

I open my legs so he can settle more comfortably on top of me. One of his hands slides up, and he tentatively cups one of my boobs, squeezing gently.

"You can be rougher than that, she likes it," Mason instructs Ben. I guess he's gotten over his hysterics.

Ben increases the pressure, and I shudder with desire, the urge to pull my clothes off and tackle him riding me hard, but I know I have to let him take the lead or I could scare him off.

"Don't think I won't make you pay for laughing at my suggestion," I tell Mason when Ben pulls back, his lipstick smeared and a dazed look on his face. "You'll be the first to feel the wrath of my strap-on."

"I'm sorry, but you took me by surprise," Mason apologizes, "and you know I'm into kinky shit, so bring it, baby," he says, wiping his thumb over my mouth. "You have a little lipstick on you. It's a good color on both of you." He looks back and forth between us, but his comment makes Ben scramble away from me.

"God, I'm sorry I shouldn't have done that." He pulls his wig off his head and brushes his hand through his own hair, messing it up.

"Why?" I ask him, sitting up, sad that his body is no longer pressed against mine.

"Look at me, I'm only half pretty." He waves a hand at his body. "And I bet my face is a mess after all those tears."

I grab his hand and stop him from leaving the bed. "Ben, I don't care either way. I said it before, but let me be clear. I like both Ben and Poppy and everything in between. If you feel more comfortable as Poppy, then get cleaned up, but I like Ben just as much." It seems like maybe young, impressionable Ben has had some major emotional damage done to him by the ultimate predator. Mabuz better not come too close to me, or I'm going to scratch his fucking eyes out.

"Really?" he asks in disbelief.

"Of course I do. I love you any way you want to be."

"You love me?" Now he sounds like he doesn't believe me.

"Of course she does, don't you feel it too?"

Mason asks, sitting on the end of the bed. "Right here," he says, pointing to his chest. "She's burrowed deep down, and there is no getting her out."

I grin at him and nod, glad that he knows what I'm talking about and that he feels it too.

"I think it's because of the mate bond. It makes the fated thing easier to accept because love is instantly there. It also makes the urge to seal the bond ride you harder. If it wasn't, I don't think demons would mate as quickly," I say. I thought about it a lot in those first days when I mated with the guys. I didn't blink twice before jumping Carter's bones even though he'd been a complete asshole to me.

Ben drops his eyes and shakes his head in shame. "No, I don't feel anything."

I glare at the hideous mark covering the spot on his chest where he should be feeling love for me, but I can't blame Ben. He was a young, naïve eighteen-year-old who was taken advantage of. "It's okay. Maybe it will happen once we seal our bond. Do you want to do that?" I ask hopefully, unsure if I'm about to have my heart obliterated or not.

"Glory is asking if you want to fuck her and see if we can override Mabuz's hold on you." Mason sounds especially enthusiastic, but I think it's as much about sticking it to Mabuz and taking one of his like he took Mason's ex as it is about Ben and me.

"Yeah, I really do. Just give me a moment." He jumps off the bed and hurries back into the bathroom.

"You know, we don't really need an audience or instruction," I tell Mason dryly, and he grins.

"Yeah, okay, I can take a hint. As much as I would like to watch what's about to happen. I should probably let you two figure this out yourself. There will be plenty of time for us to play later. Can't say I wouldn't like to see that lipstick stain ringing my cock." He adjusts himself and grins unrepentantly. Dirty bastard.

"How do you feel about him now?" I ask, and Mason shrugs.

"The kid's a victim, not a villain. Treat him well, Glory, and banish all thoughts of that asshole from his head." Mason gives me a quick kiss just as Ben gets back, his face washed clean of all makeup and still only wearing those little pair of briefs. "I'll leave you to it. Have fun," he says to Ben before getting up and giving him a quick kiss on the lips before leaving. I watch with a smile as Ben's fingers brush across where Mason kissed, his eyes wide with shock.

"I thought he hated me," he mutters, his eyes glued to the now closed door.

"He's your mate too," I murmur. "He feels that

love for you as well. He was just worried about your association with Mabuz. Mason has had his own trauma with him."

I scramble up the bed and pat the pillow next to me. "Why don't you come over here, and we can talk a little."

"Is this okay?" he asks me, waving a hand up and down his body, and I'm assuming he's gesturing to the fact that he is out of drag.

"It's perfect as long as you're happy," I assure him, and he climbs up on the bed next to me. I pull him down until we're lying face-to-face and run a finger up and down his chest. "Why don't you tell me what you like about sex?"

He blinks a couple of times, shock registering in his eyes. "What... What do you mean?"

"Well, do you like me running my finger over you?" I circle his nipple with my nail, and it puckers in response, and goosebumps break out across his flesh. He bites his lip, and his eyes get heavy as he nods.

Before I do anything else, I quickly jump off the bed. "Where are you going?" he asks, trying to sit up, but I place a hand on him to stop him.

"I just realized I'm hot and sweaty from the damn Segway. Give me a moment in the bathroom too." I lean in and give him a reassuring kiss before hurrying into the other room. I stop dead at the sheer disaster zone of makeup and hair products, but I don't want him to feel self-conscious, so I don't say anything. I just find a washcloth and throw it into the sink, turning on the water before stripping off my clothes. At first, I leave my underwear on, but then I decide to get rid of that too. He needs to be comfortable with my body, so there's no point in delaying the inevitable. I use the washcloth to wipe myself, getting rid of the dry sweat from the heat of Hell before washing my pussy. A whore bath is going to have to be good enough for today. I pull the band out of my hair and use his brush to tame it straight. Mostly happy with my appearance, I return to the bedroom. Ben's eyes are closed, and he absently rubs his brand with one hand. I decide then and there that I am going to blow his fucking mind, and he's going to learn what he likes and how to ask for it.

Chapter Thirteen

When he feels me climb onto the bed, his eyes open and almost bug out of his head.

"You're naked," he squeaks, and I giggle.

"Well, yeah, I thought maybe you'd like to touch me too." I give him a gentle nudge of encouragement as I lie down on my side, my head resting on one arm, and I continue touching him.

I can see him trying to decide what to touch first when I take the decision out of his hands. Sometimes we need a little push. I grab his hand and bring it up to my breast.

"I really like having my nipples played with. You can use your hands or your mouth," I suggest. He takes my suggestion well and runs his own finger around my nipple, much like I did for him. It tickles, but then he uses his finger to pinch one, and my giggle turns into a moan.

"That feels good," I tell him when he snatches his hand away. Surely he isn't this inexperienced.

"Ben, what did sex with Mabuz entail?" I ask him, stroking his silky skin until I get to the waistband of his boxers. I stop and raise a questioning eyebrow, and he gives me a shy little nod, so I reach beneath them and take his cock in my hand. It's hot and hard, and while not as thick as some of the other guys', it's long. I give it a stroke, and his whole body shudders as his eyes drift closed.

"Sometimes, I would give him a blow job, and sometimes, he would fuck my ass," he mutters quietly, enjoying my hand caressing up and down his long length.

"No foreplay?"

"Not really. Occasionally, he would have me suck one of his other boys off, but he was possessive of his things, so he didn't like to share. We were warned that we would be punished if any of us fooled around with his other possessions."

"You've never had a blow job yourself?" I ask, hoping he can't hear the excitement in my voice.

"No," he admits.

"Would you like one?" I ask, crossing my fingers and toes, hoping he will say yes.

His eyes open, and he drawls dryly, "I'm inexperienced, not dead, Glory." Holy crap, there's the brat. Let's hope we see that more often and not the scared victim Mabuz turned him into.

I smirk and push him so he rolls onto his back. I can be down with this. I straddle his body and lean down to kiss him, my breasts brushing across his chest. Our tongues tangle for a moment, and I bite his lip hard. He gasps.

"Be a good boy and let me know how this feels," I order.

I slide down his body, all hesitation gone. My mouth reaches his nipples, and I circle each one with my tongue before sucking and nibbling, giving them equal attention while my hand still strokes his cock. He squirms beneath my attention, and I hear him groan, which makes me smirk even harder. Placing one last kiss on each nipple, I slide farther down. My core is dripping and clenching with need, but first, I need to give this man the best blow job ever. I'm excited that I'm the first person to wrap my lips around it.

Slipping a finger under each side of his briefs, I slowly slide them down his thighs, his eyes locked on mine. I see anticipation in his gaze, making me even more excited as I get my first look at his cock.

Just like the rest of him, it's pale and slender but long. It's really going to test my blow job skills.

"Fuck, how do you tuck that? It must wrap around your leg." I want to face-palm myself the moment the words slip out of my mouth. *Fucking hell, Glory.*

He snort laughs. "Industrial tape," he jokes with a wink, and the atmosphere relaxes.

I run my tongue along the length of his cock before circling the head, and his smirk disappears with a guttural groan as his hand slips into my hair. "Oh God."

It's my turn to smirk. "You can just call me Glory," I tease before giving him my full attention. I spit on it and stroke it a few times, watching for his reaction to see where he likes to be touched the most, before wrapping my lips around the top and sliding my mouth down his length, taking him deep into the back of my throat. It takes me a couple of tries, but I manage to get a good amount in.

"Oh my, your mouth is so hot and wet." His hand tightens in my hair, like he's trying not to control my movements, but I pull my mouth off and look up at him.

"You're in control, Ben. Show me what you like. You won't hurt me, I promise, and if you somehow do, I'll pinch your leg and let you know."

I can see the fear in his eyes, and I know he's been forced and hurt before.

"There's a difference when the forcing is consensual, I promise. I like it rough, so don't worry about it."

He still looks unsure, but he nods, and I continue to suck on his cock. I use a hand to fondle his balls and slide a finger backward to push against his taint. I know I can massage his prostate like that without having to penetrate him, and I want him to be completely comfortable.

He squirms beneath me, and it doesn't take long until he starts to thrust slightly, guiding my head in a rhythm he must enjoy. He's so long, though, I have to work hard to suck and lick and let him glide in and out of my throat. I have tears streaming down my face, but no one can say I'm a quitter. I swallow, and he freezes before he drags my mouth off his cock.

"You have to stop, or I'm going to come," he pleads, and I feel a wave of satisfaction rush over me.

"I don't mind if you come, I'd love to swallow you down," I assure him, but he shakes his head.

"I don't want to stop yet," he says, holding my gaze, and I see a gleam of confidence in his eyes. I want him to know he can have whatever he wants, so I nod, encouraging him to tell me.

"Tell me what you want," I tell him, and he blushes.

"I want to taste you, and I really want to feel you wrapped around my cock." He gets bolder with his demands, and I'm stoked.

"Dinner was being ordered when I was downstairs, so we don't have a lot of time. We can leave tasting me until next time if you don't mind, but I would love to ride you now," I tell him and his eyes shine with anticipation as I crawl up his body and straddle his hips. He leans up and takes a nipple into his mouth, nibbling it while using his finger on the other one.

I sigh as a rush of pleasure tingles deep inside me. "That's good," I tell him and grab his head, shifting him from one to the other so he can give them equal love. He worships them while sliding a hand between us and trying to find my clit. I show him exactly where to touch, and he catches on, quickly finding the right motion and pressure to give me maximum pleasure. I moan and throw my head back, and I feel him grin against my breast.

"You're beautiful," he murmurs as he pulls back and watches as I rise up high on my knees, trying to notch him at my entrance. It's a struggle because his cock is so long, and he helps by placing both hands on my hips and lifting me slightly. We both groan loudly as I slide down his long length. When I'm finally seated, I'm panting.

"Holy crap, I didn't think it was going to fit," I joke, and he moans.

"Fuck, so wet and hot," he mutters, his eyes rolling back in his head.

Feeling fucking smug at his reaction, I roll my hips, and his eyes snap open.

"Oh my god, do that again," he demands, and I start to ride him like a I'm riding the carousel in Central Park. My hips roll, maximizing the feeling for both of us. I grab his hands and place them on my breasts, and he quickly catches on, massaging and caressing them to increase our pleasure. I lean in and kiss him, picking up my pace. One of his hands slips between us again, and this time he finds my clit immediately. He's a quick study, because it doesn't take long to bring my pleasure to a peak. My pussy starts to flutter and grip him tightly, and his hands snap to my hips and he takes over, thrusting up hard and fast, chasing our orgasm.

We tumble over the edge together, his movements stuttering as my pussy clamps down hard, milking him of all his cum. Our bond snaps into place as the sounds of our pleasure echo through the room. The tears of joy in his eyes match the ones in mine.

Chapter Fourteen

"Whoa!"

I throw myself back on the bed next to Ben, a grin on my face and satisfaction running through my body at the sound of his voice. It's hoarse from expressing his pleasure, and I can't help but be smug that I did that, not to mention the bond is sealed with one more mate.

"So… we good?" I ask him, looking up at the ceiling. Even though the bond is sealed, and I think he enjoyed himself, he still might say no, and I don't want him to see my heart break if he does.

"So, so good," he mutters, rolling over and draping an arm over my naked body, pressing a kiss to my shoulder.

I risk looking down at him, and he has this serene, satisfied smile on his face, but then all of a sudden, he sits upright, and the smile is gone, replaced by a look of shock.

"It's gone," he shouts, and when my eyes drift to his chest, he's rubbing the place where his brand used to be. Sure enough, the ugly red brand is gone. "Thank fuck," he shouts before hugging me tight.

"Well, shit, that means Mason was right. We are never going to hear the end of this," I drawl, and he grins and shakes his head.

"I don't care. He can taunt us for the rest of our lives, because it means I'm here and happy and with you guys and not him." He shudders, and I swear Mabuz will pay.

He flops back down, a huge sigh of relief escaping him, and then he snuggles into me.

"Hey, Ben?" There's something I want to ask him, and I guess now is as good a time as any.

"Yes, gorgeous?" he says, brushing a strand of my hair back from my face.

"Where did all that stuff come from? The Poppy stuff? You didn't have a bag with you."

"Oh, I keep a spare set of everything in my interdimensional cubby. You never know when you're going to need it," he tells me lightly, and it's exactly what I thought.

"Can you show me how to do that?" I ask him, and he sits up, taking me with him.

"The cubby? You don't know how?" He sounds surprised, and I shake my head.

"No, my mother never told us about them, and I'm not sure why. How do you do it?"

"You know, it's the one blood spell that Lucifer taught his demons, because it does help us when we move between planes." He gets up, and I watch as he searches the floor for his underwear. When he finds them, he pulls them on and heads to the bath-room. I hear him moving around in there, and the toilet flushes before he returns with something in his hand.

"Here, put this on, otherwise I'm going to get too distracted, and I'll never be able to teach you." He holds out the shirt he was wearing before, and I take it, holding it up to my nose and sniffing it.

"What's that scent?" I ask him, and he shrugs.

"Dior, Sauvage. What can I say, I'm a slave to advertising, and Johnny Depp looked good in their marketing."

I giggle and pull the shirt over my head. I'm not sure it's ever going to look right on him again, because it's a tight fit across my boobs, but he just grins.

"I do like seeing you in my shirt. Okay, so there is a spell involved and a prick of blood. The blood makes it so that only you can access it. If you want anyone else to have access to it, you add their blood as well. Come over here." He gestures for me to get up, and I crawl across the bed and join him.

He looks me up and down, the shirt is one of those tight-fitted ones, so it doesn't cover the swell of my ass.

"Well, this is going to be just as distracting," he mutters, "but no one wants to put on dirty under-wear. Okay, so to create one, you need to weave the spell and add your blood, but once that's done, you can just say the words and reach into it."

"Weave the spell?" I ask him, and he holds up both hands and draws what looks like a square in the air and then he crosses it diagonally before giving a flick of his hand.

"So swish and flick?" I ask sarcastically, and he chuckles and spins me around before dragging me in close, wrapping his arms around me. I can feel his warm back through the thin shirt and his boxer-clad pubic area pushing against my naked ass. I resist the urge to wiggle it, because I really do want to know about this interdimensional cubby crap.

He takes my hand and helps me weave the spell. We do it a couple of times before he steps back. "And you say the words, '*Verdius silaeyrun.*'"

I repeat the words a couple of times until he's happy with the incantation. "Good. Hang on, and I'll grab a pin." He returns to the bathroom and comes back, holding out a hat pin from his Poppy supplies. "Okay, so I'm going to prick your finger, and then you will weave the spell and say the words, and you'll have your own cubby."

"Okay, cool. Let's do this."

There's a sharp stab of pain as he pricks my finger, and I weave the spell and say the words just as he instructed. There's a rush of power, and suddenly, I'm standing before a gap in the dimension. It kind of looks like a ripple in the air directly in front of me. I can see this room on either side, but in front of me is an empty space just waiting for me to fill it.

"Did it work?" he asks.

"You can't see it?" I ask him, and he shakes his head.

"No, only those keyed to it with blood can."

"Well, prick your finger and come here then, and show me how to add you." I gesture for him to come closer, and he blinks with surprise.

"You're giving me access?" he asks, and I shrug.

"Of course I am. Two interdimensional spaces are better than one. You can put your shit in mine, too, if you want."

A slow smile crosses his lush lips, and he steps forward, pricking his finger with the hat pin. "You just swipe my blood across the entrance and say my name, and I'm keyed in."

"Shit, what's your full name?" I ask him, feeling embarrassed, but I don't know Teddy's and Mason's last names either. I guess it doesn't matter, because now that we're mated, they will be Luxures anyway.

He chuckles. "Well, it is actually Ben Cox, but I'm pretty sure what we just did makes me Ben Luxure. Try it." He sounds excited.

I take his finger and swipe it over the slash in the dimension. "Ben Luxure," I say, and there's another wave of power, and Ben shudders.

"It worked. Thank you. You have no idea how

much having your trust means to me." He picks up my bloody finger and sucks it clean before placing a kiss on it, and I contemplate tackling him to the bed again. "Okay, to close it, you say, '*Zulauana.*'"

I do as he says, and the space disappears, but he doesn't give me a chance to get excited before he speaks the opening words himself and holds out the pin. "Here, you need to bleed again so I can give you access to mine." I allow him to prick my finger, which stopped bleeding when he sucked it, and he takes it and swipes it across the air. Suddenly, there's a shimmer, and his interdimensional space appears, but unlike mine, his is stuffed to the brim. He grabs my hand and pulls me in.

"Intention plays a big part in this spell. You can make it appear fully like this so you can walk in and out, or you can say the words and just send things here or pull things out of it. Say I wanted to grab that wig without entering." He points to a gorgeous bright pink, long curly wig sitting on a mannequin head. "I would say the spell words and think about the wig, and I could just slide my hand in, and it would appear."

He drops my hand and starts digging around in one of the drawers. Yes, this space is fully situated like a walk-in closet with hangers, storage space, and a large vanity with excellent lighting.

"Here." He passes me a pair of his briefs before stepping over to the hanging space and pulling out a gorgeous silk bathrobe. "I only have fancy dresses in here, so there's probably not much point in me giving you one, but you can wrap this around yourself so you don't have to put on your dirty clothes. I'm sure you're probably starving. Should we go find something to eat?" he asks as he pulls out a pair of jeans, slides them on, and searches another drawer for a shirt, which he pulls over his gorgeous chest.

"You seem to have everything in here," I say, looking around, and he shrugs. "I like to keep everything in here, and I also don't have to have a permanent place of residence. I guess I was always preparing for the day when I could escape Mabuz, but with that brand on my chest, it seemed impossible."

"Are there others with his brand?" I ask as we both step out of the interdimensional space, and he says the word to close it.

"Yes, he has a stable of minions and sycophants. Some of them want to be there, while others are there because they wanted to live on Earth but they had no other options. All of them are branded with his mark. I would hate to think their only option of getting away from him is finding their mate, because there's a good chance it won't happen. Like I keep saying, he is possessive of his things and doesn't like us to interact with other demons apart from the ones he owns.

Meeting you was a fluke, one I'll be forever thankful for."

He kisses me like I'm the very air he breathes. Just when I assume we're going to try for round two, he pulls away. "Come on, let's get you fed. It's been too long since you ate, and I don't want you getting sick." I'm so touched by his concern, I feel tears well in my eyes, but I quickly wipe them away.

"Actually, we should probably look at getting you all the necessary sins you all need." How do demons deal with the need for sin when in Hell? That's something I've never asked. It's easy enough on Earth, but do demons have places they can go?

"I think being mated makes the need for sin lessen. I feel fine, but it might also be the envy that was pouring out of Mason when he was in here earlier that made me feel so good."

"He was envious?" I don't want him to be jealous or anything.

"Yeah, but it was only because he wanted to play as well. He did the gallant thing, though, and let us have our moment alone. We will have to make it up to him later." Ben winks, and I giggle.

"If you bring your bratty self to the party, Mason will be in dom heaven," I reply, and he laughs.

"I can sure try. You have no idea how much lighter I feel now that the brand is gone. I was too scared to act out with Mabuz because I knew he would punish me, and not in a fun way." He shudders, and I give him a hug.

"Never again," I promise him, my voice rough with emotion. "All punishments will be fun, consensual, and pleasurable from here on out."

"Don't be sad. I couldn't be happier, I promise. Now let's get you some food." Ben takes my hand and drags me out of the room and down the stairs.

I stop him halfway down. "Oh, there's something I forgot to tell you." I have to explain about Julian, but I have no idea where to start.

"You met your sloth mate, I know. I could feel it, remember?" He holds his hand out, and he has the final light blue ring around his envy designation as well. "How did you manage that on the trip between Nolan's parents' place and here?" He cocks his head to the side.

"Well, it turns out that Julian is my final mate," I say, and he blanches slightly.

"The gatekeeper is your mate? Holy hell," he mutters, and there's a wary gleam in his eyes as he turns and looks down the stairs.

"What does he look like? Is he big and ugly and covered in pock marks? I can imagine that's what he shifts into after looking like Cerberus."

I smother the smile that wants to appear. "I think you'll be surprised," I hedge and take the lead, dragging him down the stairs.

"But Glory, he wanted to eat me. Don't make me go down there," he whines.

"Yeah, I think you're going to want him to eat you. I know I do," I whisper so the arrogant asshole doesn't hear, but it gets Ben moving a little less reluctantly.

When we arrive in the living area, the atmosphere is no less tense than it was when I left. The TV is on, and it seems like the room is divided down the middle. Nolan, Carter, and Louis are on one sofa together, all with beers in their hands, and Mason and Teddy are sharing a sofa in the middle, also with beers in their hands. Julian is asleep in his recliner on the other side.

"Whoa," Ben mutters when he sees the ethereal beauty that is Julian. "I wasn't expecting that," he whispers quietly in my ear.

"Told you so," I reply.

"Glory, my little cream puff." Louis jumps to his feet. "There is some food in the oven for you."

"Thanks, babe," I say, but I'm interrupted.

"Hey, you French fuck, don't you take the credit for the food I organized. You're not even French anyway, so what the fuck is with the accent?" Julian cracks an eye open and glares at Louis with undisguised disdain.

"I grew up in France, you dog turd, and I wasn't taking credit, I just assumed you were too fucking lazy to get it for her," Louis retorts, and Nolan and Carter glare at Julian in solidarity.

Fuck my life. I can see that nothing has been resolved while I was otherwise occupied.

"Well, this is fucking fun... Not." I huff with exasperation. "Come on, Ben, let's leave the children." I don't have the time or energy to referee this shit, and to be honest, I'm pissed that they haven't sorted it out already themselves. I knew I should have brought Sparky on this trip. I could have had them sorted out with one press of the button and ten thousand volts.

Chapter Fifteen

I drag my newest mate toward the kitchen and much needed sustenance.

"Congratulations," Teddy says, standing up and intercepting us. He gives me a hug before doing the same to Ben. "Welcome to the family." It's super cute to watch Ben get all flustered under Teddy's attention.

"Did you have fun?" Mason wears his trademark smirk, and I wait to see how Ben is going to react. He puts his hand on his hip and tilts his head to the side.

"Sure did, Daddy Mason. Next time, you should stay, and I can show you how to please a woman." He slaps Mason on the ass and hurries away as Mason's mouth drops open in shock.

"What the fuck just happened?" he mutters, and I grin.

"I guess your brat wish came true. It seems that no longer being blood bound to Mabuz is doing wonders for our newest mate."

"It worked?" Mason's eyes widen with delight. "That's awesome. Now I get to tell him I told you so. I'm pretty sure I know exactly how he can thank me too." Mason quickly follows after Ben, leaving Teddy and me to trail behind them.

"That doesn't bother you?" I ask him, knowing Teddy is going to have to share his dom with at least one more, and I want to make sure it's okay.

He just grins and shakes his head. "Nah. Mason has enough dominant energy for all of us, and I can't wait to see Ben shake his foundations, because he's so used to my obedience. It's going to be fun."

When we arrive in the kitchen, Mason has Ben pushed up against the fridge, and he's whispering something in his ear. From the way Ben's eyes widen and then hood with desire, I'm almost certain it's something naughty and fun, but food is my first priority.

"Stop playing with him, we need to eat." I push Mason to the side and drag Ben away from the fridge. I'm pretty sure he wasn't scared, but I think we still need to ease him into this. Mabuz has left some scars, and we don't know how deep that trauma runs, but I shouldn't have bothered. Ben quickly recovers and blows Mason a kiss.

"Sounds fun." God, these men are going to be the death of me. I don't know how my mom kept track of three men who weren't interested in each other, let alone seven. Seriously, it had never occurred to me that I would have more than one mate. This is going to take some serious patience and flexibility, but I've always been good at rolling with the punches.

"Enough. I want food, and the sexual tension in here is distracting, so either stop it or take it to a bedroom," I complain as I bend down and peer into the oven. There are two foil wrapped plates, so I grab a dish towel and pull them both out, setting them onto the island for Ben and me before grabbing cutlery.

When I pull the foil back, the scent of a spicy rice dish hits my nose. It looks similar to jambalaya, but I'm not positive if that's what it's called here in Hell.

"Damn, that smells good," Ben says, grabbing one of the stools and digging into the food. Before I join him, I peer into the fridge and find a bottle of wine. I pull it out and pour myself a glass before asking Ben if he wants one.

"Yes, please," he says around a mouthful of food, and for a moment, he reminds me of one of my brothers, and I almost blanch at how young he is. But then I remember he's seen a lot in his years, and I just hope I don't corrupt him too much.

I pass him his glass and join him at the island, taking one of the other stools.

"So things didn't get any better?" I ask Teddy, who shakes his head.

"No, they can't stop snapping at one another. It's crazy. There is so much animosity. Julian holds a grudge against Nolan for leaving, and Nolan blames Julian's man-whore ways."

"Julian admitted that most of those were rumors. He said he enjoyed it when Nolan's wrath demon was close to the surface, but he didn't realize he pushed him far enough to leave. He was hoping to trigger the mate bond," I explain, and Mason groans.

"What an idiot, but sloth demons are notorious idiots. They spend so much time napping or being lazy that they aren't completely in tune with society niceties. People tend to overlook them."

"Well, whatever it is, they need to get that figured out. I don't think we should walk into Luc's palace without everyone being on the same page," I say between bites of the delicious food. It's spicy and salty and perfect for after sex food.

"No, especially because once people realize you're a septimax prime, they are going to start hurling challenges at you from all directions, and as a septimax prime who isn't completely bonded to all seven mates, you can be killed without the risk of the rest of them dying, so there's a good chance those challenges will be to the death." Mason delivers this news with a sober tone.

The food I ate suddenly feels like lead in my stomach. "Are you serious?"

"Unfortunately he is." Ben nods. "Anything goes. Weapons and magic are allowed. I remember seeing a mate challenge televised once when I was a teenager. It was a bloody mess, and that one wasn't to the death because the mate bond had already been sealed. The challenger ended up winning, and the land broke the already sealed bond. It was horrible. I can still hear the agonized screams of the loser as their bond was severed." He shudders and scoots a little closer to me. I put my hand on his thigh and give it a reassuring squeeze.

"So despite Nolan's reticence, I'm going to have to fuck Julian sooner rather than later."

"Well, as delightful as that offer is, I'm afraid it's going to have to wait," Julian drawls from the doorway. "I'm afraid time is up, and Luc has sent his guards over to retrieve us."

"Fuck. Kerry?" I ask, and he smiles at my concern.

"My sister disappeared not long after you went upstairs to 'speak' to Ben," he whispers, making stupid finger quotes, and winks. "I closed my eyes and wished her luck. I'm almost certain Luc can't see through my eyes like he does Cerberus's, but I wanted to give her a fighting chance. I know how much she isn't ready to be tied to Hell." He looks back over his shoulder at something.

Aww, that's so sweet of him. Maybe he's not a complete idiot after all.

"Crap, okay, can I finish this, or do we need to

leave right now?" I look longingly at my half eaten plate of food and hope that I can finish it.

"No! Lucifer has prepared a feast to welcome his niece and her mates to Hell." A large man pushes past Julian and seems to suck all the air out of the room. He's tall and built, a little like Chris Hemsworth, but that's where the similarities end. His skin is as dark as the sky on a moonless night, and he has long dreads that drape down his back. His shockingly blue eyes glimmer with what I'm sure is menace. He looks around the room like he's expecting to see something or someone.

"Holy fuck," Ben and Mason mutter at the same time, as Ben scrambles to his feet, and the two of them bow their heads. They obviously know who this is, but Teddy and I are clueless.

Julian just rolls his eyes and gestures at the newcomer. "This is Leviathan, one of Luc's lieutenants."

Leviathan gives up on whatever he's looking for and stares straight at me and nods his head. "It is a pleasure to meet you, Gloriana. Luc has been waiting many years for his sister to return, but he is just as pleased that you have chosen to visit. Please, if you would follow us, he is waiting for you."

Even I can hear the order in that politely worded suggestion, so I get up and then remember I'm still wearing Ben's silky robe.

"Can we have a moment to get changed?" I ask

him, and he narrows his eyes, looking me up and down.

"Fine, but you have five minutes. If you are not down in that time, I will send someone to get you."

"God, slow your roll, Levi. She will be quick, I promise." Julian glares at the lieutenant, and they have what seems like a silent conversation with their eyes.

I see Levi's body relax slightly. "Congratulations on your mating, gatekeeper. Luc is most pleased you and his niece will be linked."

What the fuck? How does he know that?

"Fucking Luc has been spying on me with his damn looking glass, hasn't he?" Julian grumbles, and Levi nods. I feel a moment of panic that he knows where Kerry is, if that's the case, but Leviathan doesn't show any sign of it.

"Yes, you know he doesn't like it when you shift and he can't see where you are. Cerberus is precious to him, and by extension, so are you. Stop being so childish when you shift and let him know where you are, or you could even move into the palace like he has asked a million times."

Levi sounds like he's talking to a wayward child, and Julian has a stubborn set to his jaw.

"You know why I don't."

"Well, maybe now that you are mated, it will be easier," Levi says cryptically, and I'm about to ask what they are talking about when I hear shouting from the front room.

"Ah, your other mates are growing impatient. Shall we get moving?"

"Fuck, you didn't leave Beelzebub with them, did you? You know Nolan's a wrath demon, and I don't doubt that sneaky fucker has probably baited him some way."

"You know Beelzebub will only be getting even for you, Jules." Leviathan grins, and Julian rolls his eyes and disappears. "He's quite fond of our friend and doesn't like how Nolan hurt him," he explains gruffly.

"Men. You're all idiots." I push past him and make sure no one is destroying Kerry's parents' place.

I find Nolan being restrained by Carter and Louis, and Julian scolding another giant of a man. This one looks like a Viking. He is tall and broad and has his long blond hair styled in two braids that hang over his shoulders. His blond beard is neatly trimmed, and he is grinning impishly at my three mates.

"I can fight my own fight, Bub. Or don't you remember the chunk I took out of your ass last time you tried to wrestle Cerberus?"

Beelzebub winces and rubs a phantom pain in his ass. "Of course I do, you mangy mutt, but you know how protective I am of my family, and you are included by default." He doesn't sound all that happy about it.

"Well, as lovely as that sentiment is, please don't try to fight my battles. Nolan and I need to have a private conversation. We all need to be on the same page now that Glory is going to the palace. You know the likelihood of a challenge is high."

The red in Nolan's eyes fades, and he settles down enough for the other two to release him.

"Yeah, Luc isn't going to be able to keep her safe for long. You better all be on the same page when the challenges start flowing, or you're fucked." Beelzebub sounds cheerful about it, which isn't reassuring.

Julian just shakes his head and sighs deeply. "Get changed, Glory. Luc will have a hissy fit if we don't hurry."

Hearing him say that makes me think that the ruler of Hell may not be so different from his sister after all. How has he managed to keep the peace for so many years? We all hurry to make ourselves presentable, but there's an ache in my heart where the final bond needs to be sealed. Hopefully we won't meet any obstacles before we can do that, but somehow, I don't think we will be that lucky.

The trip to the palace is less interesting than the one into the city. Lucifer sent a limo that's big enough to seat all of us, and of course the drive takes five minutes to circle the block to the large, ornate gates of the palace. I mean, we could have walked, and we offered, but his two lieutenants insisted we ride with them "for safety."

When we arrive, a guard opens the limo door, and we all get out. Julian mutters curses as he takes the lead, walking into a seemingly deserted palace. We follow quietly behind, none of us wanting to break the tense silence, followed by Leviathan and Beelzebub.

"Where is he? In the throne room?" Julian calls over his shoulder.

Levithan answers, "Of course he is. You didn't think Lucifer would let this go without a giant show, did you?"

Beelzebub chuckles as Julian swears a blue streak.

"If my mate ends up dead because he's decided to play games, I will kill him myself," Julian snaps as a wave of panic rolls over me at his words. Behind me, one of the lieutenants growls.

"He would not endanger his niece. I think you will find he's doing everything to ensure she is protected," Leviathan says as we stop at a set of large, decorative doors with two guards standing in front of them.

Julian has a quiet conversation with one of them, and then he steps back as they open the doors with a flourish. A guard knocks on the floor with the staff in his hand, and the buzz of noise silences.

"Please welcome Gloriana Luxure, princess of Hell and septimax prime, and her seven mates," a guard announces, the words echoing through what must be a rather large room. They both step out of the way, and Julian gestures for me to enter.

I look down at my casual clothes and wince. I have a feeling we are all way underdressed for this, but oh well.

I step into the large room and look around. At the front of the room is a large dais with a throne on it. There is a table running perpendicular to the throne with place settings and twelve chairs, but only one of them is occupied. The rest of the room has a long banquet table that must sit at least a hundred people, if not more, and all of them are focused on us as we enter the room.

The man at the front of the room stands up from his chair. I see him search our group, his eyes not stopping until a slightly disappointed look crosses his face and he sighs. He quickly hides it, though, and throws up his hand. "Welcome, my beautiful niece. Please come forward and join me."

The black-haired man is the spitting image of

my mother. It's kind of uncanny. He has the same sensual, full lips and almond-shaped green eyes surrounded by lush lashes. He's just as tall as his lieutenants but not as burly as them. He's also hot, and I feel kind of weird looking at him, and then I feel gross because that's my uncle. I wave a hand at my face, and Julian chuckles.

"Don't stress, he has that effect on everyone. Come on, he isn't patient," Julian says, tugging me in the right direction.

I stumble after him, but it's like I've stepped through a forcefield. Suddenly, a wave of magic rushes through me, and a burning sensation just above my left boob has me gasping and yanking my shirt down to look at it just as a voice inside my head says, *"Welcome, Glory. I have been waiting for you."*

I stare down at my chest, horrified to see a black mark on it much like Mabuz's brand that used to be on Ben, but Julian stops and turns, and when he sees it, he gasps and drops to one knee in front of me.

The crowd bursts into loud chatter, and I watch as Lucifer approaches me with a self-satisfied, extremely pleased look on his face.

He pulls me in for a hug. "Just go with this, and I'll explain everything to you later," he whispers before moving away and facing his court. "Hell has finally chosen an heir. Let's raise a glass and salute my replacement, Gloriana Luxure."

The crowd instantly stands up and raises their glasses. "Gloriana Luxure, long live the heir."

I look around the room at the mostly smiling courtiers, and it's a small surprise that I'm not hyperventilating. Holy hell in a handbasket, what kind of trouble am I in now?

Thank you so much for reading Glory's newest book. I know it's not some huge saga full of drama and intrigue but sometimes you just need something fluffy and I think Glory fits the bill. I'll be wrapping her story up very soon so keep an eye out for the preorder.
If you loved it, don't forget to leave a review, it helps it get seen by people.

In the mean time why don't you check out one of my other series. You can find everything you need to know here.

www.lexiewinston.com

As usual I have thanks to convey to the people who help produce my stories.

To my cover designer Tash of Dazed Designs I know it's a struggle working with me but we get there in the end.

Thank you to Jess at Elemental Editing. In the words of Kelly Clarkson, my life would suck without you.

And lastly to you guys the readers. I love what I do, and probably would do it regardless if anyone read them or not, but you guys make it that much sweeter so thank you.

Until next time, happy reading

Lexie

www.ingramcontent.com/pod-product-compliance
Lightning Source LLC
Chambersburg PA
CBHW020517120726
47904CB00003B/871